# HOTEL    PARYS

(EST: 2011)

## Taku Mkencele

**Dedicated to my parents and The Screwdriver
Genius for their limitless supply of love and support
This edition is published by Lulu®**

First (Print) Edition

ISBN: 978-1-4466-2336-7

Chapter 1

I was mixing dough for his favourite yoghurt and molasses bread when my husband called to inform me that he would rather suck on a camel's udder than come home to me. He hung up abruptly, after I told him to try the back lanes of Marrakech for a discreet sponge bath in a tub full of camel dung. I left the receiver off the hook, and got down to some serious baking while grooving to eighties' pop hits like, I should be so lucky.

Everything was perfectly fine until my mother came sniffing around the house three days later, with a week's worth of her vegan culinary nightmare leftovers.

The last thing I needed was the maternal shield that was bearing upon me. I felt her oppressive protection the instant my ears picked up the clanging of her silver, copper, and turquoise bracelets.

She let herself into the house with the set of keys Alasdair had thrust upon her before fleeing our love nest. The yellow belly had consigned the duty of finding my bloated body floating in the bathtub to a middle-aged housewife with the soul of a butterfly. She froze at the door as she took in the neatly stacked loaves that took up every available surface including most of the kitchen floor.

"Holy Vishnu, you've been very busy haven't you?" she exclaimed in the tone that genuine idiots adopt when addressing the mentally handicapped.

"Your sixth sense is on overdrive today." I replied, happily pummelling at an agreeably squishy lump of dough.

"You know that I never liked him anyway," she proclaimed, literally breathing down my neck.
*
I suddenly felt naked in my spanking new butcher's apron and paper slippers. I had little time to come to terms with the inevitable tear squeezing hug which unleashed mind-bending anguish. This uncalculated act of love set off a brief, but utterly devastating emotional breakdown. I allowed her to take over my existence as I swam amongst the dregs at the bottom of the barrel of human misery, shamelessly wallowing in self-pity. My orgy of self-flagellation was intermittently broken by blinding rages that turned everything before my eyes into a livid wall of severed limbs.

Eight mornings later, I crawled into the bathroom and wretched for what seemed like eons, sickened by my duplicitous reaction to a 'misfortune' I had willed upon myself. I scrubbed myself clean of the vomit, lint and the sticky sweat from days and nights of fitful sleep. By the time I floated downstairs to get breakfast, I was in a shiny bubble of self-satisfaction for finally fitting into my little blue dress without having to remember to hold my breath. My mother was still pottering about, so I let her fix a huge fry-up before sending her back to her abandoned husband.

"Jamie can take care of himself, you know," she said, making a concerted effort at averting her glassy eyes from my incredulous gaze.

A strung out minute tottered past before she finally retrieved the tongue she'd swallowed while squirming under my unflinching glare.

"We both think I should be here with you," she protested as I pushed her out the backdoor.

"I'll bring your basket over tomorrow." I shouted through six inches of wood, over the racket made by her tiny fists pounding against the locked and bolted door. "For poo's sake, just let me breathe for a wee while," I pleaded.

Her jewellery cluttered angrily as she finally walked away: "just remember that I tried to be here for you when you get buried under the walls of your mouldy bread fort."

She shouted expletives all the way to her car, cursing the day she gave birth to me. That was a brazen lie, since I did not spring from between her lily-white hips in the first place.

She had told me that my real mother was black, the African jewel in their Scottish father's collection of exotic treasures. My granddad was a globetrotting polygamist, an honest and attentive husband who dedicated equal time to each micro-family. He was a stickler for tradition, which was why he had whisked my Xhosa grandmother to Zimbabwe for a proper wedding. Interracial marriages were illegal in South Africa at the time, so they moved to Transkei after their honeymoon.
They had shared a thatched cottage set in an

untamed garden on the shore of the wild coast of Port St John's. She became the head of a successful woman's farming co-op who secretly produced a particularly potent strain of Pondoland cannabis. Hamish went about doing whatever it was that enabled him to be a comfortable resident and provider in four different continents.

I never met either of them, nor was I blessed with enough time with my mother. She was the hapless target of a letter bomb, and I the helpless six year-old who turned to stone. The commotion that rocked me when my mother was taken away was muffled by an angry storm that ripped the coastline apart. It was the violent nature of the weather that always lulled the village into the false security of the familiar. I was not there to be part of the collective grief, to witness the first piercing wail that actualised an immense tragedy.

We had lived in my mother's parents secluded home as part of a tight-knit community of a few scattered homesteads that were connected by an invisible bond of empathy. Kwezi was every mother's daughter, as the village had recognised when her parents were mysteriously drowned ten years earlier. A local oyster peddler had fished their rigid bodies out of the shallow end of the rock pool in the cove that used to be Kwezi's playground. She was eighteen when she accompanied the remains of Hamish and Angel McLaughlin to Stornoway ten years earlier. They were interred in the crypt he had built for any member of his family who did not find him too repulsive.  None obliged; they needed more than an eternity to live down the shame and forced isolation from the religious community they had been part of since its inception. Never meeting the McLaughlins and their not having an inkling of my existence was one of life's better bargains. Jessica and Jamie have given me two sets of doting grandparents who spoilt me with gifts and intrigued e with their rich lives.

Had it not been for them, Kwezi would have drifted off into oblivion along with the traces of my heritage.

My maternal great-grandfather had disowned Angel soon after he learned about her relationship with the foreign white boy with strange ways. His actions were not rooted in malice; he was driven by the desire to protect his family from the malevolent beast that reigned over South Africa. There was a law against what his daughter was doing; it was called the Immorality Act and he wanted no part of it. He decided that safety would be an impenetrable wall between his family and his terminally love-stricken daughter. Angel was banished from her family home and her relatives' consciousness. Her name was uttered only in silent prayers, under the covers, in the dead of the night.

With three generations of grief coursing through my veins, losing Alasdair was like having my front teeth knocked out by Bruce Lee, in an unfair playground fight. All I needed was for Jessica to back off, and let me deconstruct my five years with Alasdair. I had to have space to regress to the point where I opted for immersing myself in whatever it meant to be happy. It was vital that I pick at my past choices to move on with a clearer picture of myself, behind the fog of desires and concessions.

The part of me that did not loathe Alasdair was grateful that he bailed out of a moving car; leaving me half-asleep in the passenger seat, with a tattered roadmap on my lap. At least I had a vague idea of where I was headed, as I laid belly-up on the overstuffed couch. My mind meandered around ways of shoving Melinda into the past without causing too much of a stir. I was no longer interested in running her chaotic kitchen. I had no inclination to deal with the brain dead kitchen porters, and the vacant waiting staff. I was at the end of my chewed up tether with the lethargic pastry chef; he took an hour to plate-up a single portion of rhubarb crumble and custard.

My boss, Melinda Fern, was outwardly supportive when I broke the news of my immediately effective resignation: Inside she was a seething cauldron of anger. A fragile receptacle of a dangerous mixture of the vile emotions that well up when one is left on the lurch.

"I don't suppose you can work until I find a suitable replacement," she said, wringing her hands, which I suspected was an attempt at suppressing the urge to kick the shit out of me.

I eyeballed her warily from my end of the coffee table, "look Mel, it's nothing personal, but there's nothing, and no one that can make me go back to boiling squeaking lobsters to order for another flaming week." I replied. "Especially not in a kitchen full of nut jobs, reprobates, and waiters who think

Spain is in France."

She sucked on a phantom sour gumdrop, and then washed it down with the sweet tea I had served in dainty porcelain cups. I looked magnificent for someone that was chucking her job after being jilted on a whim.
 She swallowed more bittersweet spit.

"I can see that you're going through a hard time, but that doesn't make you less of a bitch. If you weren't such a good chef, I'd strip down to my knickers and dance with joy at the prospect of never having to put up with your put downs for another day." She said.

"You'd have to spend a fortune on liposuction if you want to do that without losing face." I replied.

"I'll be off now," she announced in a measured tone, looking like she'd just been winded by the incredible hulk. "For the record, fuck you," she added before slamming the front door shut.

I tidied up the tea things, ruminating on the fact that the only friend I had was a bleary-eyed heiress with an addiction to anything she can get her hands on. The only thing she was good at was breeding Shetland ponies. That is what she did when she was not terrifying Jesus out of anyone that strayed into her perpetual carnival of hedonism.

I imagined that her parents christened her, Thumbelina, hoping that it would add an allusion of daintiness to her towering frame. The six foot two raven-haired beauty carried her name like a sabre, daring anyone to acknowledge the joke without her permission. We guided each other through university, and she helped undo most of the damage caused by my childhood traumas, relocation, and agoraphobia. The latter was probably a result of my home schooling by a pair of socialist-vegan-anti-nuclear power protesting-pacifists. My aunt/mother Jessica and Jamie, the only father I'd ever known, showed me immeasurable love and treated my mind with respect. They would have made magnificent teachers had the education system not been designed to breed intellectually arrogant morons, and celebrity obsessed freaks that believe and lust after everything they see on the goggle box.

A retrospective take on everything made me realise that Thummie and I had no other choice but to bond. We were too big and too smart for imprisonment in a caged community of drunken students with shallow expectations, and no clue that complacency is a privilege.

She was the only other person besides my family that knew of the moment my world was shattered in a cataclysmic explosion that only lasted for only half a blink. Alasdair had always assumed I'd been adopted from a Jamaican orphanage, and I preferred that to having a relationship that would be driven by pity. As for Thummie, the story of my family triggered her aborting the quest for the source of the psychopathic tendencies, which plagued her despite her fairy tale princess upbringing.
After becoming my chief confessor, she promptly made the assertion that the world was crazy; that was the end of her relationship with the homely

shrink who chewed ceaselessly, consuming tons of roasted pine nuts throughout their ten years of fruitless banter.

My reverie was cut short by the banging on my front door; "what the fuck do you want now?" I yelled.

"Just one blow job and I'll be off," Thummie replied in a manly voice.

"I thought you were that crazy bitch and her degenerate army," I explained as we made our way to the kitchen.

She pushed past me, started rummaging through my drawers, and then turned towards me brandishing a corkscrew, "get us a couple plates please."

"Would you also like some knives and forks for your wine?" I said

"Just the two plates thanks, but a pair of glasses would add a nice touch," she flashed a Hollywood white smile.

I looked at her properly for the first time since she'd arrived. She looked normal enough in her riding breeches, wellies, and a totally inappropriate sequined top under a knee-length hooded raincoat. I managed to get some plates without turning my back to her; I feel edgy when unhinged people waltz into my home making peculiar demands. I made a point of setting the plates on the table with extra care, "there you go," I grinned uncomfortably.

"Take a bloody seat, and stop looking at me like that." I settled down to watch as she emptied the contents of her grimy mackintosh' pockets onto the kitchen table. I inventoried a jar of honey, six liquorice sticks and a box of dinner mints, four tea towels, a bottle of lemon and honey salad dressing, and a set of tiny pink cashmere booties.

I buried my head in my hands and moaned, "Please tell me you're not having a baby."

She held her tummy protectively, invoking a maternal glow that sent shivers down my slightly bent spine. I shuddered involuntarily as I imagined the fate of the unborn child that would be reared on the mad woman's love.

"Just kidding; I couldn't resist having them," she explained while serving the stolen fish.

"Don't you think you're taking this shoplifting therapy thing too far?'" I was in perpetual awe of her criminal vices; I loved her too much.

"Do you want some of this lemon thing with your fish?" she asked in an eastern European accent.

"So, what's the lady's plan?" she asked after we had finally relieved the table of all the edible weight, accept for the booties and the fish oil stained kitchen towels.

I studied my hands, "I think I'll start growing my nails again, and then I'll figure out how to get where I wanted to go before I got derailed by that pinworm." I still couldn't say his name out loud.

She stroked the tip of my nose with a fishy finger, "The best way to make sense of your world is by getting absolutely pissed with complete strangers," she said.
We sat in silence listening to the boiler and the creaks of a house going about its day to day life.

I took her advice to heart and headed out on a solo whisky tasting bender that lasted for a bit more than two weeks. My pursuit of alcohol-induced clarity was a trek that stretched across the highlands to the Western Isles. I spent restful nights in cosy country hotels, lost in cheese and port dreams as my soul ran backwards through broken walls.

All I had on me was a satchel that contained a few clothes, my toiletry, and the bank card that would pay for more clothes, transport, and lodgings. I was beginning to enjoy occasionally bumping into some of the tourists I had met and befriended along the distillery trail. Which is exactly what happened when I was on the high street in Pitlochry staring at a golliwog display in the post office window?

"Oh, Ceilidh, you must have tea with me," Leonie literally dragged me into a teashop after spotting me through the window.

We'd only just met the day before in the smallest distillery on the planet, when we were both high on cask strength Eduardo. We had fallen about laughing at a private joke about AA meetings for seraphim that had gotten hooked on the angels' share. The tour-guide had a difficult time trying to subdue us. We were like best friends on a primary school field trip, which was a new experience for me because I had skipped that part of my childhood. Later on we dined together and drank until the wee hours of the morning in the tiny bar of the Moulin hotel. We attracted the company of a bunch of wild pensioners on what seemed to be their final road trip. I could not get out of bed in time for breakfast because of a blinding hangover, which prevented me from bidding my new friends a proper goodbye.

"I thought I'd lost you forever," Leonie told me as we settled down for a pot of tea and scones with jam and clotted cream. Craig nodded vigorously while his wife Wilma patted my hand across the table. That's when it dawned on me that I had imposed my hard-luck life story upon complete strangers during my weak moments of drunken self-pity. It was then that I remembered that the deluge of shock and distress had been triggered by Wilma and Craig's talking about their lifetime together, and the beloved country hotel that had filled the void of their childless union.

"Wilma has something to tell you." Leonie's eyes had the incandescent glint that's usually associated with a generous morning tipple. Her breath was an overpowering mixture of Fishermen's mints and Pernod, which made the offer she was making on Wilma's behalf seem even sweeter.

"Wilma and Craig are looking at buying a canal houseboat down south; they were wondering if you'd like to buy the hotel since you were weeping over the pictures last night." She glanced at the ageing couple and then turned to me. "Take some time to think it over and I'll ring your mobile in a couple of days," she suggested.

There was no way I'd pass up the chance of buying a quaint little hotel in the pastoral landscape Wilma had described in such detail. Especially not since they were asking for a little less than what I would get for my bungalow. I couldn't resist an opportunity to start over in a quiet pocket of rural South Africa. It would be like moving to the countryside in the south of France without having to overcome a language chasm.

"I'll take it," I accepted in case they changed their minds. "I'll need some time to sort out the finances and I'll want to spend a month running it before finalising the deal" I added, grinning back at the beaming couple who had just given me the perfect opportunity to pick up the pieces of my life without having to lean on Jamie and Jessica.

Jessica could not contain her relief when I informed her about my decision to spend a year in Parys. She pulled me to her bosom. "Thank Vishnu; you're not going to rot in that bungalow after all." She yelled for Jamie who was in the living room, preparing a defence for another protester that had been arrested for streaking in the Faslane nuclear submarine site.

"This had better be good," he moaned as he settled onto one of the stools set around the curved breakfast counter.

Jessica kissed the top of his head, "our little angel is selling that awful bungalow and she's buying a hotel in Paris from a batty old couple." She spoke through a mouthful of hummus and organic olive ciabatta.

He asked her to swallow, and got up to give me a tight squeeze. "Please don't leave me alone with this crazy old bat," he pleaded.

"Go fuck yourself Jamie," she responded with decades of affection in her throaty voice.

The mock altercation made me realise just how much I would to miss their colourful banter and the love we lavished upon each other with great crudeness.

"Take care of each other you two," I said, battling to control a stream of tears. "About the hotel, it's in Parys, between Johannesburg and Bloemfontein, in the middle of South-African nowhere."

They exchanged looks, and for the first time in my life I couldn't read their conversation. "What was that about?" I glowered at them. They both shrugged feigning ignorance, and I decided to let their sly exchange slide.

We sat up all that night reviving the past and planting seeds for the future. I spent as much time with them as I could in the weeks preceding my departure. It was a futile attempt at staving off the prospect of being more than a short drive away from my security blanket. They had given me life when all I'd had to cling on to were the vivid images of my past in pieces. It wouldn't be easy to open another door to the rest of my life so far away from them. There was much fanfare when Thummie drove us to the airport in her family-size off-road vehicle. The cab was a hot box; Jamie kept rolling and passing joints around throughout the ninety minutes long journey to Glasgow International. The mushroom tea Jessica had made us all drink before leaving the house added an ethereal quality to the countryside that was slipping back as the car sped forward. I promised to set up a blog spot so they could keep track of every minute detail of my imminent adventure.

**Chapter 2**

There was no-one to meet me at the Johannesburg International airport, and not much point in moping about it. I could afford the three-hour long taxi ride at the ludicrous exchange rate. I felt all pervading sadness when I was supposed to be jubilant at the conversion of my decent sized packet of peanuts into a hefty pile of wealth. I traced it to customs officers who were red-eyed and ashen-faced to a man. They looked as if they'd just seen the ghost of a favourite uncle impaled on the nose of a Concorde. Airline agents were sobbing openly, clinging to each other seeking comfort in the folds of each other's silky blouses.

"What the hell is going on?" we all wondered amongst ourselves as we started feeling the weight of the funereal mood that rippled across Customs. Then the terrified old man that was behind me on an electric scooter started muttering about a coup. That caused a stir of panic amongst the sun-starved Brits. All conversations took a sharp turn towards the possibility of being marooned in the airport. The young hippie couple behind me brainstormed a protest strategy; just in case they failed to elicit a refund from the travel agent who had sold them their bargain-bin tickets at the last minute. In spite of our fears, not one of us asked the sullen customs officers if there were streams of blood running down the motorways and byways of the city of gold. The crestfallen faces that met us at the arrival terminal were further evidence that South Africa's people had just survived a collective collision with the devil and his demon cadres.

"Why is everyone so upset?" I asked the only taxi driver who was willing to drive me all the way to Parys.

He regarded me with miserable eyes and replied, "Joy Khanya was snatched from her driveway this morning; her little boy witnessed the whole thing." He sighed and turned away to load my bags into the boot of his brand-new Toyota Camry. He ushered me gently into the backseat of his car since my legs had turned to jelly and my heart to pulp.

"Who is Joy Khanya?" I asked feeling like the ignorant Westerner I had tried so hard not to become. I also couldn't help feeling irritated that the violence that had driven me off had not been consigned to the pit of eternal fire along with all the other relics of South Africa's soul corrupting past. He adjusted his rear-view mirror for a better visual of my dumb arse.

"She is a symbol of hope to millions of young South-Africans that are eager for make their mark in the world. She is also the most powerful campaigner for the Social Democratic Movement; a strong voice against the new wave of classism, and a proponent of people friendly capitalism." He replied.

My obviously microscopic knowledge of world affairs reduced me to a pinhead in the spacious backseat. "Why would anyone want to kidnap a government minister?" I asked as we turned onto the motorway.
He chuckled heartily, even displaying the appropriate

shoulder-heaving action.

"Strange," I thought to myself, "abduction of a confused politician is not that funny."

He continued explaining despite the confusion on my shiny face: "She's not really a politician. She's a community activist who won Big Brother Africa two years ago, and she's never looked back since. She's endorsed every green product under the sun. Has spoken on campuses from Thohoyandou to Tokyo; she's the Lara Croft of green politics and a thorn on the ruling party's side."

I couldn't make sense of what he was on about and I made that implicitly clear.

"I'm sorry," he said. "So, you're a fellow big brother hater?"

"I'm not following you," I stammered, frowning. "Is this my last taxi ride?" I asked myself.

I went back to feeling like an arse when he said, "I'm surprised you don't know who she is because she won your country's Celebrity Big Brother last year." It was my turn to burst out laughing.

"I vaguely remember seeing tabloid headlines about the awesome curves on an opinionated African girl," I said.

"That girl is the body, face and voice of our cyber-space and television-crazy youth are beginning to associate with the future. She simplifies everything from foreign policy to little infringements on freedom of speech dressed up as a means of protecting the public against perverts."

Thomas, the taxi driver, was a human chatterbox with a malfunctioning stop button. By the time we reached my new home, I already knew everything there was to know about current socio-political affairs. He had an encyclopaedic knowledge of modern history, and was a natural at cross referencing relevant information from his monumental store of data. His face was a grim mask focused on the road ahead, convincing himself that the day's events were just the tip of the iceberg of conspiracy and orchestrated mayhem.

"We are headed for dangerous times"' he observed glumly.

"Trust me to go seeking tranquillity in a land that's on the brink of turmoil," I muttered, not realising that I'd vocalised my inner conversation.
Our eyes locked in the rear-view mirror and he said, "Don't you worry, us ordinary folk will be too caught up in the daily grind to feel the heat of change."

My stomach went ice-cold, despite rising bile and the thick heat that blew in through the open windows in piercing gusts. "The fact that people aren't aware that the ground is shrinking around them does not mean that there won't be panic when they finally realise they've been trampling on each other to stay alive." I commented in a stricken tone.

He nodded and replied, "Let's hope that we don't live

to regret the mistakes of a few."

The mood in the car had grown oppressive so we tried to lighten the load by exchanging stories of our roots. I learned that Thomas was once a successful shopkeeper until a major grocery chain moved in on his newly paved Soweto neighbourhood. He could not compete against the monopolies that control the production and distribution trail.

"The people now believe that not having to travel too far to reach a chain store is as much their right as having equal access to the ballot box," he explained, shaking his head. "They forgot that they were fighting for the freedom to earn their future off the land, and not to be blind consumers in the free market."

I amused him with my family history of polygamy, inter-racial breeding and Christian fundamentalism. Speaking to Thomas openly came naturally to me; it was my first breath of fresh air after a decade of living in a submarine. When we lugged my bags over the ivy-framed threshold, we did so as friends. We forged ten years worth of loyalty in an hour and a half of relating our lifetimes in bullet points.

"Can I help you?" said a gruff disembodied voice from the unmanned bar.

I'd been told stories of haunted old colonial manors, but not once in my life had I considered that I'd someday be spooked by an Afrikaner ghost; I turned to Thomas and pointed at the bar.

"'Did you hear that?" I asked.

"I'm over here, dear," said the thing.

I dropped my bags and jumped out of my skin as it touched my elbow with its furry tentacles. "Holy Vishnu, you scared the life out of me," I shrieked at the diminutive woman who was still prodding me with a cobweb duster. I offered her my hand as she walked towards me.

"I'm Ceillidh," I said to the goggle-eyed midget.

She regarded me as if I were a piece of the moon that had just plummeted from the heavens onto her rubber sandaled feet. I on the other hand was flung aback several miles by her bizarre choice of outfit. The Boy Scout uniform, knee-length socks and sandals fashioned out of car tyres were at odds with the greying, immaculately groomed figure with a boyish frame; she was also eyeing me out with matching abandon. She beat me to regaining composure.

"'I'm Alana, I didn't expect you to be so black," she told me in her froglike voice.

"Pardon me?" I replied, looking to Thomas for backup but he just chuckled to himself with his arms folded against chest like a schoolboy watching the early stages of a drunken bitch fight.

"Wilma said you're Scottish." The suspicion in her eyes translated into the hostility in her hardening voice. I'd had enough of her nonsense: I fished my passport out of the back pocket of my jeans and practically threw it at her.

"Would you like a cup of tea Thomas?" I asked.

He just grinned at me like a wax coon while the cross-dressing midget carried out a careful inspection of my passport; they had pushed me too far.

"I need a shower and some food and you two can get tae fuck," I growled in the thick Glaswegian accent that plagues me in moments of intense rage.

The outburst cleared the air like a spring breeze scented with orange blossom. Soon the three of us were seated in the conservatory, engaged in polite conversation over a pot of tea and fresh koeksisters. The sun had gone down by the time Thomas headed back to Johannesburg with an outlandishly large tip. After all, he did promise to return with paying guests. Alana went back to preparing dinner for Mr Wilson, the only guest in the hotel.

It was a sprawling Cape-Dutch farmhouse set on an immaculate lawn bordered by neat rows of yellow and red tulips. A long gravel driveway stretched from the gate along the side of the hotel to an ivy covered wooden gate marked "Service Entrance: Please Don't Park in Front of the Gate". A wide pebbled footpath bordered by lilies cut across the lawn from the middle of the driveway to the front stoep.

I dragged my tired body down the steep stone paved path leading to my new home at the bottom of the lush green grounds behind the hotel.

*The stone cottage had a slate roof and a glass canopied stoep that wrapped around it. The living room's wooden floor was covered in a faded blue Persian carpet and the stone walls were softened by large brightly coloured bushman art inspired wall hangings made from hemp. Normally I can't stand wicker lounge furniture; but it looked right in there. I promised myself I'd get rid of the floral cushions as soon as I could find something better online. I had a modern home office instead of a dining room, which was fine by me, considering that the kitchen table could seat an entire battalion. The best thing about the stone cottage was the traditional farm kitchen that oozed postcard charm. The walls were crawling with an assortment of herb hanging baskets, and the wooden shelves were filled with rows of neatly labelled jars of a myriad of pickles and preserves. Wilma's collection of leather-bound hand-written recipe books stood proudly on a single shelf that ran the length of a wall. Some dated back to the days of Krotoa, recounting the tale of the creation of Afro-Dutch cuisine and its first brush with the oriental zest of the Malay slaves. It's a fragrant history with hints of ginger, cloves and cinnamon. However, the best thing about the cottage was that nature was never out of sight because one side of the walls is a glass sliding door leading to the thatched stoep.*

That's why I couldn't help but sit on the battered wicker rocking chair staring through the trees, at the full moon trapped in the waters of the stream that ran through the grounds. The soothing sound of flowing water rocked me into a peaceful slumber, but I was rudely awoken by the chilly breeze of the witching hour. I felt grubby in the clothes I'd been sweating in for over twenty-four hours.

My heart sang an aria when the creaky old taps of the deep freestanding tub poured out a steady flow of steaming hot water. My sore muscles stayed in soapy-suds heaven, until all I could think of was getting my shrivelled arse under the quilt Alana had laid down earlier.

I took to cycling around the tiny town seeking inspiration on how to attract trade to the beautifully kept Hotel. I went on most of the cycling and walking trails, talking to lone anglers and then passing out with exhaustion on the banks of the meandering streams. They were laid out like jewelled bands adorning the gentle curves of the green land.

The town centre was another story altogether: It had the haunted feel of a long forgotten one horse town waiting for time to keep tumbling onwards. Grand old buildings looked on at the local council's on-going battle with potholes and equality issues. This included introducing nineteenth century conveniences like tarred roads, and street lights to the black township that was on the outskirts of the town.

The main street was overrun by bakeries and home industry stores with the same safe selection of merchandise: mostly milk tarts, rusks, and marmalade. Every other shop sold second hand furniture; these were manna to the urban antique-hunters who stood out like glowing thumbs in the dark during their weekend invasion of the sleepy town. They seemed to have agreed on a uniform of oversized shades and simple tees. The women wore blue jeans accessorised with men in designer cargo pants. These super cool couples strutted up and down the main road snapping up bargains, most of their finds were artificially aged furniture pieces that were cooked up by shrewd rural tradesmen. I couldn't help but salute them for their deceptive methods of sating the influx of wannabe collectors.

"Why don't any of the weekenders ever sleep here?" I asked Alana when I returned from another day of eavesdropping on pointless conversations about television adverts and random first person reports on sexual indiscretions.

"Why don't you ask them?" Alana growled at me, gnashing her dentures at the mere thought of looking after the dreaded city people.

She was agoraphobic and best suited for the dual role of head housekeeper and cook, considering that she had never left the grounds since 1986 and had no inclination of doing so. I on the other hand was dying to breathe new life into the hotel.

"I'll be doing more interviews next week," I said, feebly feeling for firm ground as everything sank around me.

"Like we need more mouths to feed," she stormed off and slammed the kitchen door shut, leaving me to deal with the half prepared meal for six.
Business was slowly picking up due to the aggressive advertising campaign Thomas had

helped me devise. It's amazing how creative the mind can be when one's evenings comprise of playing twister with Alana, and then passing out drunk and spent in her sweltering bed-sit.

Her room was right next to the kitchen. It had a rarely opened glass double-door overlooking the back garden that provided the kitchen with most of our herbs, bulbs, legumes and roots.

**Chapter 3**

Thomas had given me a six weeks deadline to have the place looking and running as it should. One of his regular fares was a lifestyle editor for a perfume laced woman's magazine that contained three kilos worth of foundation and shampoo samples. He had promised her a free romantic weekend break with all the trimmings in lieu of a write-up. Her name was Megan; she called to confirm that she would be sharing a room with her photographer, warning me that she had to tell it like it is. I thought she should just be thankful for the romantic bonking setting and all the free food and booze she'd be stuffing down her pipe.

At that moment I was willing to sell any one of my limbs to have the beds occupied by living beings. As for Alana, she would have to get used to the fact that the hotel was much more than just her home. Wilma and Craig had treated the business like a hobby, it seemed like all they really cared about was keeping the hotel. The guests were merely a part of their social lives, and for Alana they were fodder for the illusion that without her the fortress would turn to dust. Which is why she had to remain in charge of the new help or she would not know what to make of herself amidst all the changes. The idea of transformation undermined all that she had grown accustomed to and I knew that the only thing that kept her there was sheer lack of alternatives. It was time to either "adapt or die", and neither of us was quite ready to throw in the towel yet.

She returned, wearing a fresh layer of kohl and rouge to cover the tears that were still clinging to her eyeballs: "How many new people are you going to force down my throat?"

"Only three to help you with the housekeeping and service; you can keep Koos on as the gardener even though he won't say a word to me." I replied in a syrup coated voice.

Koos was a racist old git, but good jobs were hard to come by and so were good tomatoes. He was water and the hotel was fish; without him there'd be no claims of scrumptious meals made from freshly picked produce. Alana's face lit up, "you should see the size of the mangoes in the greenhouse." She chatted excitedly while I fantasised about homemade creamy mango mousse with a drizzle of passion fruit syrup.

## The New Arrivals

All three of the new staff arrived on the same day. Justina, the polish girl was the first one in. Thomas dropped her off just in time for breakfast. I couldn't risk having Alana scare her off on her first day, so I took it upon myself to show her to the staff quarters. I'd had the double storey cabin erected a hundred meters away from mine a week before the staff's arrival.

*The cabin had a wooden deck overlooking the stream. It had glass sliding doors that opened into the kitchen. Which was a modest built in unit with a fridge, a hob, and oven; I had even thrown in a microwave, toaster, kettle and a waffle-maker. The rest of the bottom floor was a large living room with every modern entertainment gadget a spoilt city brat could dream of.*

Justina looked around with the glee of a rural child on her first visit to a toy shop. The new TV/DVD combo in her room proved to be the climax of her first day with us. She sang praises to my thoughtfulness in stilted English until my stomach churned. I suggested she wash up and join us for breakfast and then bolted back to Thomas for more news from the real world.

"He took a sandwich," Alana explained his sudden disappearance with superficial indifference.

I gulped down my disappointment, "I suppose he can't hang about since he still has two more to pick up for one-thirty."

She buttered every inch of her toast carefully saying, "Well aren't you the rocket scientist today?"

She beamed at my irritated face, displaying her new set of permanent dentures. I wanted to knock them off her gums with the silver teapot, but Justina's sweet face emerged from behind her just in time. Introductions went down pretty well despite the random insults that went right over the girl's head. Alana watched her wolfing down the massive breakfast.

"She looks more like a Turk than a Pole to me." She observed.

I suppressed a giggle; the girl did have suspiciously dark curls and a Mediterranean complexion. I think I said, "Alana will teach you everything you need to know," and then I exited to pick up an imaginary phone-call.

I couldn't just sit there, dribbling a gooey mixture of egg and suppressed mirth down my chin. When I returned Alana announced that breakfast was officially over. She loaded everything onto her trolley including our half eaten meals. Justina started to complain but a strategic kick on the shin turned her protests into agonised yelps. My job was to reinforce these new bridges and I would be screwed if I messed up the foundation.

Thomas dropped Abe and Lucia off at the same time because there was only an hour between their landing times. Abe was an eighteen years old Amish boy on a two years overdue, once in a lifetime freedom binge before returning to an existence of cultural isolation and the rigid rules of the Old Testament. His curly ginger fringe covered his eyes, and his freckled cheeks turned crimson at the slightest hint of embarrassment.

Alana gave her heart to him the moment she laid her eyes on the boy. It was going to be amusing watching the old bat's heart flutter every time the lad flicked his fringe aside to smile at her. Lucia's crush on Abe was more devastating than Alana's; she hardly touched her lunch for staring at him as if he was the only nourishment worth hankering after. My latent maternal instincts were tweaked by the crush-stricken, fragile girl with a friendly pug-face that turned to pudding when she smiled. She was supposed to be twenty-three but didn't look a day older than fifteen; so skinny she was growing fuzz on her skin to keep her bones warm.

"I don't know if she can handle making those big beds," Alana commented after taking one exasperated look at her.

The mouse turned out to be a wildcat; "I'm much stronger than I look," she hissed at a stunned Alana. "Anyways back in Valencia I work in building sites during the summer."

Abe's Amish manners failed to hold in his girlish laugh; he had a fruity double hand wave to go with the high pitched giggle. I'm still not sure if I was laughing at him or at Lucia's ludicrous testimony to her toughness.
She could be frightening when she's upset, which was why I made a mental note to try not to ruffle her fuzz in future.
Alana on the other hand had a look that suggested the beginning of all-out war between her and the fiery Spaniard. She had low tolerance levels for fussy eaters: I did not need to read tea leaves to know that Lucia's micro biotic diet is going to brew many storms.
Thomas ate quickly and made his excuses, he was out the door and on the road before I could get up to stop him. He seemed more preoccupied than he usually was; I'd had no opportunity to poke my nose into the entrancing space between his ears. I concluded that it was me he's avoiding, and not the traffic he claimed to be dodging by skipping the

customary pot of tea in the conservatory.

 It may not be the most spectacular room in the farmhouse, but I it was the ideal spot for catching up with paper work while indulging in a healthy fix of curtain-twitching. The window seat made for an acceptable table if I sat on two overstuffed-cushions with tacky gold tussles. From my low makeshift workspace I could see as far as the road beyond the borders of the property. Koos kept his hedges trimmed so low, I could see legless cyclists' bodies hovering past like giant praying mantis. Being beneath eye-level meant I could see most of the action on the grounds without being spotted. It helped to know what's coming down the driveway. It gave me the edge in beating Alana to the cafe that used to be the under-utilised reception lounge.

I was weaning her of her habit of misusing the room's spooky acoustics; she enjoyed giving guests and day trippers the spine chilling welcome she had given me. The dark prank dampened the experience of stepping into the magnificently illuminated room.

The steadier flow of lunchtime trade had Alana and me merrily slaving away side by side in the large farm kitchen. Sometimes it was like being in hell: with all the heat from the gas cooker and the oven that was almost a head taller than I am.
Justina would rather scrub all the toilet bowls in the world with her fingernails than cook on a hot afternoon. She claimed that the kitchen was once the devil's furnace.
The arrival of the extra hands meant that I was free from trying to do everything at once. My days of

sweating like a cross-country runner with hyperactive sweat glands were over. My main concern at that moment was making sure that Megan and her "photographer" have a brilliant time, and hopefully lots of sex. There would be nothing to fret over had I not agreed to cater for a wedding party of forty city people on the same weekend. When I took the booking I wasn't aware that both families-in-law were certifiably mad.

The bride and groom to be had stopped by for lunch on a whim when they fell in love with everything; you'd think they'd never seen fresh bread-rolls and butter-curls before. How could I have denied the puffy-eyed bride her wish after she'd professed that the hand of fate had guided her to the manor?

"It's perfect; please say yes," she had whined disarmingly. "Tim and I can get married in the garden and, we can have the reception lunch in that lovely conservatory."
I couldn't eke out the courage to crush Eliza's fantasy. Especially after she'd said, "Tim's parents are catholic but I was raised in the Dutch Reformed Church. My parents would prefer seeing me in a porn flick over marrying in front of a catholic priest."

 The young couple's catholic versus protestant sectarian dilemma made me homesick for Scotland. I was incapable of denying them the perfect temporary solution to the lifetime of melodrama that would be the inevitable fly in the post nuptial ointment. The thing is, three weeks of Eliza faxing and ringing me with continuous setting suggestions and menu changes had left me with an overwhelming desire to wring her neck before her mother-in-law could get to it.

My workers were cloud's silver lining, their ability to make me laugh shortened the days. Abe was a hit with everyone he comes in contact with; even grumpy old Koos was taken in by his charm. They were quick to form a fragile kinship that stemmed from their love for the soil. Their easy interaction was marred by Abe's intolerance of Koos' acidic brand of bigotry that dripped onto everything within his reach. Not even his favourite pair of garden shears was exempt from the vitriolic monologues he muttered under his crowbar moustache from sunup 'til sundown. Most times I got a whiff of the stench of his quiet rage as it festered undisturbed by time and the erratic flow of life.

### The Wedding Rehearsal

Eliza and her posse had arrived unannounced in a fleet of shiny off-road vehicles during lunch service; the cafe was full to the very last table. I was in my own zone picking herbs in the back garden when Lucia stumbled out of the kitchen at high speed, calling out my name at the top of her voice. Her arms flayed about as if to feel out for me, having gone blind with panic.

"Kay-lee Thank god you're here." She gasped, tugging at my sleeve like an impatient toddler on the check-out queue of a toy store.

I shrugged her off and got on my feet, "Where the hell did you expect me to be you silly cow?" She shrunk away from me contorting her pug face as if she was anticipating a painful blow. "I'm not going to hit you."

She straightened out her face up, "your wedding people are running amok on the grounds, and the crazy mother-in-law is throwing a fit at the bar." She gave me an imperious once over and said, "maybe you should clean up first. You're all filthy and greasy." Her emphasis on filthy gave me the impression that she was referring to much more than just my dungarees and the frizzed-up afro that was sprouting out of the top of my turban.

I nearly sprained my foot sprinting down the stone path for a quick improvement. By the time I'd finished reconstructing my appearance Abe had managed to contain Eliza's rampant flock in the conservatory. He had one pile of plates balanced on the crook of his left arm and another on his hand when he gave me a quick briefing on the situation. He also had his right arm around a highchair, and an empty gravy-boat clung on to his fingertips by its sticky handle.

"Thanks wonder boy," I gushed, unable to give him a cuddle without injuring both of us: I ruffled his ginger hair instead. Incredible reach is one of the scant perks of being a head taller than your average man on the street.

"It's a pleasure darling," he shouted back in a phoney redneck drawl before disappearing into the kitchen.

I donned my invisible armour and marched to the conservatory with a mad monologue ringing in my head. The invaders were seated in a loose ring formation on the floor sipping timidly on mango juice that could've been spiked with mild sedatives.

Tim's mother (Magdalene Simmons-Smythe) was the first to spring to her feet. "Give me one good reason why I should be wasting my precious leisure time in here, when I could be at my book club?" she huffed.

I took one good look at the middle-aged Cindy doll in a vintage black Chanel suit and all my nerves went on overdrive. She reminded me of all the posh ladies that patronised me with sickening pity when I used to cheer Thummie on from the side-lines in her dressage days. Her parents were always away, and I had to drive her trailer. I spent my Saturday afternoons amongst people that figured me for a refugee from some strife torn region of Africa. They gawked and consoled intermittently, never forgetting to marvel at my grasp of the queen's tongue.

Without these uppity enforcers of unwritten social laws: there would be no cotton boom, not much use for slavery, no ban on hemp growing, and definitely no seven years old seamstresses making Tommy Hilfiger jeans and Dunhill polo shirts.

This unfeeling fringe of humanity made me realise why older non-Europeans are so obsessed with "looking presentable". It is for the upper classes' benefit that black people and workers everywhere have been conditioned into believing that only tramps, druggies, white students, absent minded professors, and eccentric moneybags can look however they please.

Magdalene Simmons-Smythe was from an era when well to do English speaking girls were locked up in exclusive schools until it was time to go to university in search of a mate of the same social standing. Her Voice Clinic perfect intonation had a grating effect on me; I wanted her out of earshot as quickly as possible.

"Maybe you should discuss that amongst yourselves because I haven't a clue what you are meant to be doing here." I said.

The room drew a collective breath of disbelief. All fifty-six eyes turned to Eliza. Even her groom had a dark look of fury about him; you could see him counting the runs of televised cricket he was missing.

"We are getting married two Saturdays from now, and we haven't rehearsed anything yet," Eliza said in her own defence. Everyone's eyes turned to me for some freakish reason known only to them.

"There's nothing to rehearse; you're being wed by a rented clerk under that peach tree over there," I pointed at the abnormally large tree that stood proudly on the neatly trimmed front lawn.

Magdalene turned on Tim, "Timothy, I cannot believe that you didn't hire a proper catholic priest."

Yvette Van Zyl, Eliza's mum, cleared her throat to

speak but I interrupted. "Mrs Simmons-Smythe when was the last time you attended mass?"

"What does that have to do with anything?' she snapped back.

"For starters, you don't just rent a priest. If these two want a catholic wedding they'll have go to mass regularly, and attend months of some pre-wedding catechism lessons." I replied.

An engorged vein suddenly popped up on the centre her forehead separating it into two neat halves. "According to who?" she hissed.

"The Vatican," I replied with a wide, smug smile plastered on my sun kissed face.

Yvette did not try to interrupt this time; she was clearly having the time of all her god given nine lives. Mannie Van Zyl and Paul Smythe exchanged brief congratulatory nods disguised as a mutual acceptance of an inevitable truce. Deeper in their minds they were gleefully engaged in the arithmetic implications of an intimate wedding in the countryside.

"What's going to happen to the vintage Bentley I was going to rent?"
She shrieked as the wedding planner crossed her mind, "Felipe Saunders is going to strangle my social life to death." She sounded truly terrified.

Paul Simmons-Smythe picked up his cue and said, "That's one less imaginary wrinkle for the laser surgeon to deal with if you ask me."

His wife turned a livid shade of red, and Yvette gulped down a mouthful of juice to make way for a raucous laugh. The floorboards shook as her ample bum wobbled along with the rest of her cream cake and chocolate pudding stuffed body.

Paul turned to Mannie and said, "That frikkin Felipe makes a hell of a killing out of bored suburban housewives."

Mannie nodded vigorously; his head bobbing up and down like a hip-hop head on speed. "A woman with nothing to do should not even know what a credit card looks like. This wedding planner business is just an excuse to give someone else your hard earned cash so they can spend it on orchids and French looking waiters." He added his two cents in his hypnotic, well- schooled Afrikaans drawl.

"I don't see how we could possibly rehearse having a three course meal," Yvette reasoned.

Magdalene responded by springing to her feet and gathering her side of the family- she shepherded her dazed flock to their respective cars with the ease of a veteran general conducting a scheduled fire drill.

"Will you give me a lift home?" Paul asked Tim, who was standing beside him with his nose pressed against the window. I watched them watching Magdalene's motorcade snaking its way into the road behind the hedges. At that moment I wanted to like them so I could offer them all a strong cup of tea, but all I could think of was how I wished they were out of sight and beyond earshot.

I cleared my throat hoping to draw Eliza away from her mother's outsized bosom; my exaggerated cough fast tracked her regression into the suckling stage.

"I think it would be better if everyone went home," I suggested just as Justina popped her head in to announce a minor sauce emergency. "Brilliant!" I thought to myself as I seized the moment and walked them to the driveway with a tight grin. I also hinted that Magdalene could do with some Hormone Replacement Therapy before the wedding.

As for the strawberry and mint sauce, I had a surplus hidden in a beetroot salad container. That's just one of the implements of deception I had to employ to keep my sweet toothed staff from consuming the meagre profits of the pudding menu. I felt like a new-age Mother Hubbard every time I had to throw them out of the still-room to keep them from seeing my hidey-holes and camouflage devices.

**Chapter 4**

I leapt out of bed with a start because the sky had come alive with electrical energy. In fact there was enough lightning to turn every wild grass arrangement in all the designer urns in each suburban household on the planet into kindling for the fire of Armageddon.

I had grown accustomed to the random thunderstorms, so it was not the incessant clapping of gigantic hands that blew me out of deep sleep. I'm no explosives expert; but I was dead sure that I'd heard a series of bombs going off not too far away from the hotel. I scanned the sky for smoke and listened for emergency sirens for over an hour, but there was still no confirmation of carnage.

Breakfast was like an emergency intelligence briefing in a top secret bunker of the world's major spooks; everyone felt the dodgy manmade rumblings behind the predawn thunderstorm. That's everyone excepting Koos; he had confided in Abe that he had slept through the fracas like a new-born baby after a frenzied feed. He claimed that living in this valley for half his life enabled him to sleep through the worst lightning storms. Abe believed Koos knew more than he was letting on; but then again Abe spent half his free time staving off Koos' company. The old man's ultra-right wing attitude was too much for the boy to stomach: He also had a habit of drawing parallels between the Amish way of life and his dream of an independent white state. His ideal of a racially pure utopia for god's chosen people was a constant source of trauma for Abe. He had enough trouble working out why it was taking us so long to realise that half the things we did to each other on a daily basis were just wrong.

"I have a strange feeling about him," Abe told us when we were tidying up the still-room after lunch service.

I'd never spent more than a minute around Koos; so I could not add much weight to Abe's observation. Justina and Lucia would not even go out to pick a tomato if Koos was about. We left it up to Abe and Alana to worry about what the gardener meant by what he had not said. I didn't have the time to invest in unravelling the conundrums that came out of the mouth of an ageing bigot. At least that's the reason I gave for not joining Alana and Abe on their jeep ride to reconnoitre the valley for large craters and scorched ground. She would follow him to the ends of the earth if it weren't for her bad knee.

They returned with no evidence of any violent disturbances on our pastoral surroundings; even though she insisted that the adjacent farm has grown an enormous patch of mature Rose bushes overnight. Abe took some pictures with his first camera ever, which was quite impressive considering it was one of those digital gadgets with five different buttons for the same feature. We printed out the photos and passed them around during dinner; everything looked normal. Alana insisted that the sounds in the night were a portent for some evil that would pass through the valley.

Justina raised her temporarily split mono-eyebrow, "We are trying to have a pleasant meal here; it's not a fucking séance you know."

Her first dates with every single guy in the district were paying out priceless dividends in the language stakes. All our eyes turned to Alana, whose khaki kit and waxwork-perfect make-up seemed even creepier compared to the mysterious appearance of an acre of flowers. She shifted around uncomfortably, "What are you all slobbering at me for?" she snarled, baring her eerily regular, unnaturally-white dentures.

Lucia coughed out the chunk of char grilled pork she'd been choking on, "tell us your story." she spoke hoarsely her eyes pleading with Alana not to blow her top off just yet.

Alana clicked her fake teeth and said, "well: I asked Jan Marais about the noise- he told me to mind my own blooming Hydrangeas; and then he shut the door in my face."

There was a lot of self-conscious teetering, which turned into foot-stomping hilarity when Abe said, "I would have done the same if you came knocking on my door with half-baked theories and thinly veiled accusations."

Alana flinched away Abe's offensive remark, "you tell me why he looked like he hadn't slept for seven nights in a row," she reasoned, outraged by her sweetheart's outburst. "I'll tell you something for nothing, that crazy fruit bat has been up all night doing the devil's work." She added with chilling certainty.

Justina picked up her plate and stormed off to the kitchen to consume her gargantuan portions of pig flesh in peace. She's on the Atkinson diet; it keeps her lithe, pallid, and vaguely putrid.

"Good; my brain was suffocating from the stench of musk and rotting cow," Alana whispered as the girl wafted away from the conservatory.

My mobile phone vibrated in the breast pocket of my dungarees, so I excused myself and scuttled off to the private dining room. It was Thomas ringing me from a pub in Soweto to tell me that he might have found my family.

"What do you mean by might have found?" I asked `him in an ungrateful and imperious tone; his extended absence was beginning to gnaw at me. He told me that he'd been making inquiries on my behalf, and had finally unearthed someone that knew someone that knew my grandmother.

"Thanks a lot Thomas but some old pal of yours hardly qualifies as a long lost uncle, especially since the only genetic link between us is a shaky alcoholic flashback featuring my grandmother." I yelled into the mouthpiece, feeling as ungrateful as I sounded. I wasn't about to start biting my nails to their cuticles over some he said she said business.

"My drunken childhood-friend still lives three houses away from your great-grandfather's house. You call me tomorrow and tell me when I can take you there." He barked into my ear and hung up.

I danced around the room like a fairy on MDMA for about five minutes, and then hopped the rest of the way back to the others. They barely noticed that I was hovering several inches above ground; that was okay with me. I didn't want to start telling tales because I would start believing in them. That would be harder to recover from than falling flat on my face if I discovered that Old Mother Hubbard's giant boot had long lost its sole. Don't get me wrong, I loved the idea of hooking-up the severed blood ties, but I must admit that three generations of no communication make one hell of a gap. The notion of my role in filling that void left me feeling more inept and insignificant than ever before. My mind was on calling Thomas first thing in the morning to set up a date for Sunday. The only way I could go through the night without falling to pieces worrying about what they would make of me was that maybe I would find a bit of Kwezi in one of her aunts and cousins.

I filled the days that followed Thomas' phone call with as much hard labour as I could to make the nights shorter. During my frenzy of activity I stumbled upon Wilma's business plan for a range of organic condiments and pickles while clearing out the barn. It got me thinking that I might just get it going and see what becomes of it. It would be a small dent on the little nest-egg that was left over from paying off the hotel and the generous cash gifts from my parents, Thummie and both sets of grandparents. I submitted the plans for converting the barn into a production area to conserve what was left of my sanity.

The planning inspector

I received a call from the town planning office; I had to be at the town hall by eight o'clock the next morning for a meeting with Nicholas the planning inspector. We went over Wilma's plans and he assured me that the project seemed feasible. He gave me the details of a health and safety inspector I could consult with on what I needed to do to satisfy all the regulations. He was quite helpful and attractive, that's if you like the dark-skinned type with salon perfect shoulder-length dreadlocks and a big shiny BMW off-road vehicle. I might have accepted his invitation to dinner if he hadn't imposed an inspection of his car upon me as he walked me to Craig's old Landrover. I felt smug driving it because it was powered by a hydrogen generator. I proposed that he pop in for lunch whenever he's down our way, but that hit a bum note with his expectations.

He looked puzzled when he said, "Why won't you go out with me?"

It was my turn to be taken aback by the size of the man's ego, "that's probably because you haven't asked me out yet. Even if you had asked I would have turned you down; the only thing we have in common so far is the future of an old barn," I replied.

He flicked back his locks, "how could you possibly know that?" he said, holding the door open.

"Well let's see," I said. "You're too suave to use your full name, and I'm just way too picky to date the first eligible flashy bachelor I meet; that's if you are single."

He gazed at me with diminished affection, "I'm sorry you feel that way because I'm considered quite a catch."

"I'm glad to know that you'll have no trouble getting laid while you're doing your bit to annihilate mankind." I said, jerking my head in the general direction of his car. His eyebrows did a double jump and his Face went blank. I heaved myself into my chariot and slammed the door shut. He came along with it, his chin connecting with the soft top of the dependable hunk of metal with a satisfying thump. "Never hold on too tight when someone's trying to shut the door," I warned him as I negotiated my way out of the parking space and away from him

"You should have been nicer to him," Justina chided me after I had shared my encounter with her over a sneaky joint in the orchard.

"Give me one valid reason besides that he has to okay the barn conversion," I replied, balking at the idea of offering myself up to the local god of town planning.

She rolled her round brown eyes back and said, "I can't think of a better reason for you to flatter him than that." I took a long drag and passed the funny cigarette back to her.

"Pretending that a piece of shit is a lump of nutmeg is not how you get by in the real world," I said.

She coughed smoke into my face then she shrieked

at me, "What the hell are you talking about?"

The vapours from her gut mingled with the pleasant stench of marijuana as she gawked at me: I made a mental note to always keep my nose a safe distance away from her mouth.
I exhaled a swirling cloud of smoke then glowered at her. She smiled, and I forgot her halitosis because she looked like an exotic bloom in the fading light under the canopy of the apricot trees.

"Why do you play with every boy that shows you his toys, when you can easily sweep Superman off his feet?" I asked with genuine concern.

She lit a cigarette and shrugged her bare shoulders, "nothing beats the first date." she teased dryly as she led the way back across the clearing to the hot kitchen. "You should consider Nick for a bit of fun; you work too much." She scolded me as I trailed behind her on the lane between the cabbages and the beetroots.

I laughed out loud and then proceeded to lecture her about the perils of bathing in scum for kicks. She turned around to ask if she looked okay because we were almost in full view of Alana, who was definitely stealing glances out the window.
The steel worktop we use for chopping vegetables is under the window from which you can see everything from the vegetable patches to the orchard that created a screen between the staff quarters and the hotel.

"Just go," I hissed impatiently. My mind was

paralysed by my fear of Alana's wrath, and how she would express it if she got a whiff of reefer from my person.

"Seriously though, do I look fine?" she persisted.

"Your eyes are bloodshot, and your cheeks are much rosier than usual." I snapped as I pushed her along past the thyme.

Alana's larger than life silhouette was clearly perceptible as she moved about along the retractable wooden podium. I had a sneaky feeling that the otherwise useless contraption was built into the wall beneath the window strictly for the diminutive cook's benefit. She was surprisingly inoffensive when we made our timid entrance fifteen minutes late for our shift. We were as stoned as two surfers in a bong smoking convention.

"We have an extra four fat mouths to feed; get your skates on and bring me some orders," she hollered half-heartedly.

It was Abe and Lucia's day off, which left Justina and me to do the service and all the other tasks that "two-handed" Alana could complete without extra hands. We served three-course meals to over two-dozen people in a record two hours, and then we retired to the conservatory to feast on leftovers and catch up on daily gossip.

"Abe and Lucia are still not back," Alana, informed us for the fiftieth time since we'd started discussing the potential repercussions of my heartless rejection of Nicholas. I just couldn't take anymore of Alana's pining and the Polish girl's twisted logic. Sometimes I wondered if she'd had to flash her legs at Russian soldiers for extra lard and vinegar vouchers.

**Chapter 5**

I couldn't get a wink of sleep from twitching all night because my mind was alive with full colour audio-visual clips of the experience I'd had that afternoon. Thomas picked me up just after breakfast and immediately launched a moan about the traffic for almost two hours. We stopped at a service station with a Boeing 747 mounted on the roof.

"Do you want anything?" he addressed me directly for the first time since we embarked on our journey.

"Bottled water would help," I replied while inspecting the red panic spot that was growing on the tip of my nose. He sighed and left me to pick away at my nose as my anxiety welled up, seemingly uninhibited by the fact that my heart was pumping out air bubbles. He found me doubled over against dashboard clasping my chest when he emerged from the shop ten minutes later.

"Try breathing slowly," he whispered encouragingly, massaging my back with a soothing hand. My personalised panic attack survival manual came rushing back to me just when my mind was about to shut down from a dire lack of oxygen. "Next time try sucking on your thumb before you have a heart attack," he chuckled when I was out of the woods.

I laughed off my inner tension, "I haven't had a panic attack in ages, not even when Alasdair dumped me over the phone."

He made an empathetic whistling sound and then

asked, "How did you find out about the thumb sucking cure?"

I looked at him with ill-masked revulsion and replied, "It's hardly a cure is it? It's like saying breathing into a paper bag is a miracle cure for hiccups." He coughed and straightened up, staring straight ahead.

I mumbled my response sullenly, "I stumbled upon this novel way of calming myself down when I was thrown out into the big world for the first time at seventeen. I was around a lot of unfamiliar people for the first time after a stretch of home schooling by a pair of regular offenders of public peace laws."

He hummed an old fashioned deity and I continued sucking the skin off my thumb as we drove through an architecturally challenged suburb with an identity crisis. That's when Thomas slipped into his tour-guide persona.

"This is Eldorado Park." He said.

I took the therapeutic thumb out of my mouth and replied, "It's a nice name for a place that looks like a mixture of a middle-class suburb, and a battle-ravaged council estate in the heart of Srebrenica."

He shook his head morosely and sighed, "It's the crazy politics of inequity once again." He explained that during Apartheid it was an area that was once exclusively populated by mixed race people, and black people that beat race classification criteria by bleaching their skin and straightening their hair.

I took my thumb out of my mouth to say, "What exactly were the benefits of leaving their families and living a lie? From where I'm looking whoever was doling out privileges didn't throw much their way.'

He slowed down and told me to take in every detail of that environment and store it in my head for future reference. We went past three blocks of neat suburban bungalows, then an open field that could have been a beautiful park. The stretch of green was a no man's land separating the comfy bungalows from the stark cluster of decaying flats. These government blocks were built on even concrete ground that served as both parking lot and cheerless playground. I sighed as I took in the neglected spaces between the islands of relative affluence and the sea of poverty contained in compact little boxes that were stacked atop each other.

"Don't feel too depressed they've gone shopping for designer labels where the rich people shop; their kids are playing the latest console games on plasma screen television sets in their hi-tech sitting rooms," Thomas grumbled. "The problem is that poor people are duped into believing that credit is the mainstay of upward mobility. They use their houses to secure mortgages for: cars, leather couches, cable television, and expensive entertainment systems that cost the Chinese military industrial complex almost fuck-all to produce."

I rolled my eyes at his sermon, and continued staring at the satellite dishes that shimmered under the sun on the roofs of most of the houses. Even the mangiest homes had borrowed the portal to trash television; I was transfixed by the power and reach of the merchants of celluloid fantasies.

"This is Kliptown on your left, and the half-hearted effort at green keeping on your right is the Pimville golf-course."

The deserted green wasn't half as interesting as the chaos of the human traffic milling around the stalls that sold: toiletries, vegetables, beans, pulses, live chickens and cheap Chinese fashion.

"This is where the Freedom Charter was drafted, it's the birthplace of our constitution," he orated in a monotonous Texan drawl that had me in stitches despite the weightless tumour that was flourishing in my stomach.
"We are almost at your aunt's house," he spoke in his normal voice.

I held fast to the seat to steel myself for the recoil as my heart lurched forward.

"You said we are going to my granny's house," I whinged, outraged at being misinformed because the only other alternative was to pee in my pants.

His wits were fixed on the traffic and the unpredictable passenger pick-ups made by money-chasing, road-hogging mini-bus taxi drivers. He only responded after we had turned into a quieter side street, "I didn't mean to mislead you, but I'll leave it to your mother's people to explain the complexities of their internal relations."

I rolled my eyes skywards saying, "what's there to explain? I'm a second generation Afro-Celt and the only reason why I know sweet nothing about my African heritage is because my Xhosa grandma was amputated from the family tree long before I was conceived."

The car turned left into a cul-de-sac and stopped outside a pink house in a brick paved yard. The only green life was in the form of miniature palm trees in large terracotta pots that formed a kraal around freshly varnished garden furniture.

"Very nice, don't you think?" Thomas made pointless conversation while hesitating at the front door. I shrugged sullenly, pushed past him and knocked louder than I'd intended to. My aunt Rosemary had a face like thunder when she yanked the door open. "I'm not interested in Jehovah and L Ron Hubbard- and I've had enough of bloody pyramid schemes," she barked at us before slamming the door in our terrified faces.
We just stood there trying not to breathe too loudly; staring at the brass knocker we both feared to touch. The heavy wooden door opened again- this time around a young woman with a dazzling smile stood before us as if summoned by magic.

"I'm sorry about my mum; she's pissed off 'coz she thought she'd won the lottery." The girl smiled sweetly and rattled on as she led us into the living room. "She psyches herself up for a windfall every Saturday night: then she crashes back to reality on Sunday morning- that's why she froths at the mouth, and curses god until the sun goes down."

Aunt Rosemary was nowhere in sight but we could hear her bashing pots and cutlery in the kitchen.

"It seems like today's not a good time for a family reunion," I said, wearing a long face as I lowered myself onto the proffered couch. The girl grew even more excited and then she raced to the kitchen howling for her mother. Moments later I was being fiercely hugged and covered with wet kisses by the surly woman that had shut a door in my face minutes before.

"You look more like your grandmother, but your eyes are your mother's" she whispered after studying my face intently through the film of tears in her bug eyes.

I doubted we'd come to right house because my mother's eyes were exactly like Rosemary's and nothing like mine. She like Rosemary had been elevated from popeyed freak to rare beauty by the lushness of the curly black lashes that made an alluring canopy over her bulging peepers.

I inhaled deeply to silence the ringing bells in my head, "you may have seen a picture of my grandma because she left before you were born, but how would you know what my mother looked like?" I asked unaware that my innocent question would make her flinch and turn blue in the face.

Eve excused herself then scuttled off towards the same direction she had gone earlier, leaving the three of us to suck in the silence while contemplating the next move.

Rosemary decided to take the gauntlet, "Your mother was an interesting woman; my world grew bigger after I met her. We spent two weeks together in Harare during the independence concert," she said, staring at her fingers. I wasn't sure if she was just shy or concealing a lie. I counted back and decide to give her some credit because Kwezi would have been pregnant with me at the time. She glanced at Thomas- then she reached out to brush a stray hair off my forehead. "Chance put us in a situation that made it imperative that we know each other." she replied cryptically.

Eve breezed back in bearing a tray of tea things and a plate of cinnamon biscuits. "So, tell us more about you," she said to me. She seemed totally oblivious of the static in the air as she doled out the tea, cookies and a smattering of pleasantries. She was the perfect hostess with a refined way of coercing people into being sociable. Her chocolate skin was velvety smooth and her almond shaped eyes the colour of cinnamon. Her teeth and eyeballs were so white I could swear she'd ever seen the insides of a smoke filled coffee shop. She settled down beside me and said, "I'll show you my Miss Teen crown and my modelling trophies if you come up to my room, you can bring your tea."

I felt like a giant limp piece of lettuce sandwiched between Eve and Auntie Rosemary. I emptied my cup and got up to my feet in flash, "I'd love to see your stuff," I declared chirpily.

The bubble-gum pink walls of her room sent shockwaves from my eyes to my brain, which caused my stomach to turn violently since I was already feeling queasy. It was already too late when Eve finally had the sense to point me towards. The cream carpet in the hallway and the MTV doormat in her room were soaked in brownish sludge with bits of the tomato and egg sandwich I'd had for breakfast. She ran out of the room with her hands on her head screaming, "oh my god," over and over again.

"I'm sorry," I gurgled before doubling over, as a projectile shot out my burning mouth splattering the yellow walls with vomit. I kept my hands on my knees until a wave of relief washed over me, only to look up and find Rosemary standing at the far end of the hallway with her hands on her hips and her mouth agape. The panic returned followed by another torrent of puke, which by then was mostly water with splodges of what I thought to be stomach lining.

"Thomas! Get her out of my house now," Rosemary screamed.

I was so terrified I forgot to breathe and ended up a heap in a puddle of my own sick. They carried me to the backyard and gave me the mud caked dog treatment with a power hosepipe. When I came to my clothes were soaked and my hair was stuck to my face, neck, and shoulders.

"Thank god you're alive" Eve's sigh of relief was marred by the disgust on her mother's face.

Thomas wrapped a faded yellow towelling robe around my shoulders and led me out the side gate to the car. "Aren't we going to say goodbye?" I asked through my chattering teeth.

"Don't worry about that, I'll send you an e-mail tonight," Eve spoke from behind me spooking me right out my skin.

We hugged goodbye at the front gate then Thomas and I set out for Parys. She stayed on the sidewalk waving back at me until the car turned the corner. He turned the heating up for my clothes to dry, but the windscreen misted up and we had to wind the windows down. I squeezed between our seats into the back and knelt behind the driver's seat to get out of the wet clothes and into the relatively dry robe. He didn't utter a word until I slunk back to my seat.

"Good thinking, I was worried you'd catch pneumonia." He grinned.

I groaned and turned the radio on. I was extremely mad at him yet couldn't pin down a lucid reason for the transference of wrath, nor could I explain the irritation that was gnawing at me from being around the man that was meant to be my best friend under the southern skies. I refused to speak to him, not even after he'd tucked me into my bed with a steaming bowl of Alana's exquisite oxtail and spring onion soup.

The next morning I received an email from Eve:

*"Hey sugar*

*I'm sorry about mum's appalling behaviour; she's been going through a lot lately. Her department is understaffed, and she can't chase foreign currencies like other medical professionals because she still has to work off the degree and extra training her employers had paid for. Don't worry about the mess you made earlier; she would have reacted the same way if you'd mistakenly dropped a raisin on the driveway. I'm sure you noticed that everything is either white or yellow, and that every upholstered surface is covered in dust repellent clear PVC. Thanks to you, she's now surfing the net for a quotation on the same stuff for every inch of carpet in the house. I've made it clear that she's not touching my room. Next time you come over you can puke on her squeaky floors and then flee to my desterilised environment. She never enters my room, she can't even bring herself to touch my door handle since the day I deliberately handled it with sticky fingers; I was seven years old. That's the day she imposed a lifetime ban on peanut butter and honey sandwiches. As far as she knows it's been eleven years since a jar of honey has crossed the threshold of her shrine to the goddess of bleach and scrubbing brushes.*

*I'm sorry about the moan, it's just that mum drives me mad most times. She feels really bad about how she reacted, but as I've already explained; there's really nothing she can do about it since she's ruled out seeking professional help. I almost forgot to tell you that your friend has been here for the past three hours; I wonder what he sees in my mum. They've*

*been huddled together behind closed doors in the living room whispering stuff to each other. You better warn him about her though, she's a ball cruncher.*
*Hugs and kisses*

*Eve"*

**My response:**

*"Hi Eve*

*I'm really sorry about this afternoon; I haven't lost control like that in ages. I'm more concerned about your situation because I can handle the odd unwelcome panic attack. You on the other hand are only nineteen yet you seem to have so much to deal with. So if you ever need to talk, you know where to find me.*

*Love*
*Ceillidh"*

**Chapter 6**

Lucia dragged me out of bed kicking and screaming sometime after breakfast: there were men building a gazebo on the front lawn. I slipped on a wrinkled pair of dungarees over my pyjamas, brushed my teeth, and grabbed a tweed porkpie hat from the hat stand to cover my bone-dry frizz. The gazebo was already half erect when I got there so I laid in on Lucia,

"Why the fuck didn't you stop them?" I yelled, fuelled by frustration and sleepiness.

She squared up to me and insulted me in Spanish, "We're not paid to walk around the estate, that's why we didn't notice them until a few minutes ago. If the fat one didn't come inside to warm up his bacon sandwiches they'd be finished by now." She added demurely

The workmen stood around on tenterhooks staring at what they assumed were the early stages of a bitch fight.

"Stop drooling and dismantle that thing, right now," I screeched at the stark raving loony guerrilla carpenters.

The fat one inched closer, "sorry lady, but we have to finish before lunch; we have another job to do."

Lucia and I exchanged glances then she turned to them, "Do they even know you're coming?" she sniggered. The fat one told the others to get back to work.

"I'm not paying you; case closed," I roared hoarsely in the fat man's face.

He led his hands up in mock supplication, "Calm down lady, I've already been paid for this and I intend to earn the cheque," he smirked.

I decided not to argue with the delusional foreman and walked away saying, "Right then, you do as you please. Do convey my gratitude to the gazebo fairies for adding value to my property." Lucia was hot on my heels muttering insults that would make a sailor blush.

"I don't know, and I don't give a runny shit," was my response to all the questions Alana and Abe threw at me as I raided the bread bin for any croissants that had survived breakfast.

"Don't talk to her when she's hungry," Justina advised them on her way out.

She was on a mission to check the public dining area for imperfections that could rouse Alana's latent demons. They skulked about acting busy while I prepared a tray of warm croissants with honey, and a pot of rooibos tea. I made a run for the conservatory with my feast, knowing full well that Lucia would render the verbatim report they were gagging after. I was just savouring the lemon and honey aroma of the reddish gold liquid when Eliza rang to tell me that she had sent me an e-mail at nine o'clock to warn me about the builders. I aped her giggly high-pitched voice and said, "They were almost done by the time our cocks crowed. Nonetheless thanks for the relentless waves of thoughtfulness, goodbye."

I hung up before she could respond, and then forced the cold croissant and tepid tea down my constricted throat while sorting through the day's correspondence. There was a message from the town planner confirming that he would be doing his inspection the very next day! As if that was not enough my inbox was clogged up by several identical irritating messages from Eliza:

*"Good morning*

*I'm sooooo excited about Sunday; I can't believe we're finally getting married! I want the pictures to look perfect that's why I paid some guys to build a gazebo so Tim and I can stand there with the notary and the string quartet. I hope you like it; it would be a shame to take it down afterwards.*

*Kisses*

*Eliza"*

I punched my forehead several times after reading Eliza's message, not realising that the overweight foreman was watching me. He was standing on the now complete gazebo admiring the skilful work of his three sweaty sidekicks. He waved at me, and started jumping up and down all over the wooden platform like a gargantuan Rumplestiltskin. He then marched across the lawn, and stuck his head in my face through the open window.

"It's as steady as an elephant," he informed me breathlessly.

"Thank you, goodbye now," I said, and then I picked up my tray and left the room as fast as my size nine feet could carry me. Abe and Alana were still sitting at the kitchen table gutting fish for Thursday's pickled fish lunch special. "Do we have any bookings for lunch?" I asked in a grossly ingratiating manner that made Alana scowl viciously.

"Don't try to play nice because I know you know that you have no excuse for not turning up this morning," she clucked at me from behind an awful pair of diamante studded sunglasses.

I leaned across the table to kiss her forehead, "I'm sorry Alana. I see you scored Liberace's diving-goggles on E-Bay." Abe giggled from behind the ginger mop that covered most of his face. "Keep your ginger mane away from your face and out of that fish. I think you'll be better off with a haircut because I'll mow it off if you can't control it," I warned him in the nicest way possible.

Alana seized the opportunity to take a swipe at Abe, "What could you possibly know about Liberace when you've never even seen a gramophone, let alone a fucking record?"

Abe pecked her on the cheek and she broke into a smile that outshone the midmorning sun. "We're going down to the stream for a bit of recreational fishing," she announced, still beaming like an inebriated baboon on a Marula tree. They left me to do the rest of the gutting as punishment for shirking off my morning duties.

Lucia and Justina came back from their break to tackle the slow and thin trickle of lunchtime trade. There was a bit of swearing when a French hiker complained about the strong taste of cardamom in her special cappuccino. Justina accused the irate customer of ignorance, citing that: had she bothered reading the menu properly she'd have realised that "special" cappuccinos contain cardamom amongst other things. Needless to say the hiker left without paying, threatening to report our shocking service and grossly inflated prices to the Lonely Planet website. Justina escorted her to the door yelling, "Don't forget to tell Lonely Planet that you only turned nasty after you'd gobbled up a tasty three-course meal. Frankly you are welcome to say whatever you want if that'll save us the trouble of dealing with scum like you."

 Luckily the only people that witnessed the scene happened to be the grateful family of six that weren't penalised for checking out two hours too late. I tried apologising to them but ended up in a teary-faced heaving pile on the settee next to their table. Their faces froze then their jaws slackened; the family experienced varying degrees of horror measurable by the amount of food on their chins.

Justina leapt into action, smoothing things over like a seasoned pro, and then she marched me out of the room stopping short of boxing my ears. With our last weekend guests gone and no new bookings, we took the rest of the day off to have cocktails on the new gazebo.

"Shpringbok," Justina slurred as she gave Lucia a shot of crème de menthe and Cape Velvet Cream.

Lucia gulped the lurid concoction down, "what else have you learnt from slapping Afrikaans beef?" she asked sourly.

Justina's army of suitors were another chink in Lucia's armour, next to the unsightly dent caused by Abe's constant flight from her progressively desperate advances. Alana was the buffer between the boy's innocence and Lucia's single minded intention of bagging the ultimate virgin man to deflower her. She had read the Karma Sutra from cover-to-cover preparing for the lucky candidate that would start her off on her fall from grace. She could no longer resist the lure of the flesh, so she negotiated a trade off with god to spare her the retribution for the mortal sin of fornication. Abe on the other hand was too tipsy on freedom to notice Lucia's padded push-up bras and low cut tops.

"Why don't you eat proper food for a change? You might even pad up a bit," I said from out of the blue.

Justina started poking at her own belly, "If I gain any more weight I won't be able to see my feet," she replied.

Lucia gave me the evil eye, which turned green when she addressed Justina. "The only fat you're gaining is the cholesterol around your heart," she sniped, but her deliriously drunk adversary laughed off the insult.

"Does anyone want a blow-job?" Justina asked just when Abe and Alana climbed up the steps behind her. Abe coughed and she turned around giggling, "It's really good: try it," she added coyly.

He didn't need much coaxing to catch up with the cocktail drinking. Alana opted for less messy stuff: brandy and coke with a hint of lime juice. The story of the trip to my aunt's house carried our laughter into the small hours of the morning.

Alana was the only one up when I finally made my way to the hotel, blurry eyed and cursing the fact that the only edible thing in my fridge was a lump of Thai ginger I'd picked up on a whim during my last shopping excursion to the city. We nodded salutations to each other and went about our personal business in complete silence.

"You always have to find a way to ruin things don't you?" Alana shouted at me from out of the blue.

She stormed off into her sleeping quarters, leaving me dumbfounded and vulnerable. I emptied the blender into a pint glass and gulped the smoothie down in one fluid swig. My vital organs must have been as dry as the Kalahari in winter; I could feel the path of the cool liquid coursing down my insides.

I was on my third glass of the stuff when the service entrance buzzer went off. I picked up the intercom in the kitchen and leaned closer to the monitor for a better view of the figures in the driveway. I was mortified to see Nick's impossibly-groomed face filling up the monitor. "Hullo, we are from the town planning office," he announced smoothly; I tried to wipe his face off the screen in a moment of temporary madness.

"What are you doing?" Abe asked. His voice made me jump squealing like a pig in the slaughterhouse. The intercom's receiver went flying against the wall.

"Pick it up for Christ's sake," he said.

I had left the thing dangling uselessly while contemplating an escape route. Justina was half a step behind Abe all the time.

"One moment please," I spoke into the thing in a manly voice. I started to speak to Abe but he cut me off.

"I may have fornicated, but I'm not going to add lying to my growing list of sins." He informed me sternly.

It was at that moment that Alana's door burst open. She came out flying and parked herself between Abe and Justina like a referee breaking up a particularly nasty boxing match. "Harlot." she hissed at Justina. The girl flinched instinctively inching towards the door while casting furtive glances at Abe over Alana's head.

"It wasn't her fault Alana," he pleaded with his geriatric platonic girlfriend.

Alana was having none of it, "he was a decent boy; you had no business corrupting him," she sobbed.

I caught Justina's eye and signalled for her to come with me. She walked round the table creating a wide berth between herself and Alana, and then we were in the hallway giggling with our hands over our mouths.

"You have to hold my hand through this; I can't handle it on my own." I said, pointing towards the entrance.

"I can't talk to strangers in my pyjamas. Who are they anyway?" she asked; stifling a yawn.

Her roughly cropped hair was sticking out in all directions and she still had a bit of eye make-up on, which made her look sexy in a sleazy sort of way. Her pink cotton pyjama bottoms were crumpled up, and there was a suspicious looking milky stain on her black lace vest. I didn't look any better in the old, bottle-green spaghetti-strap dress I'd worn on wedding day a long time ago. If they were taken aback by our dishevelled state, they hid it well. Nick had little time for small talk, which was fine by me because I was in no mood to fight off his slick advances.

"I suppose you'll want to see the barn," I said coolly, and then I led the way wordlessly towards Koos' domain. I usually didn't venture towards the wild field beyond the barn and the greenhouse unless I really had to; that was my way of avoiding unnecessary contact with Koos.

"Ouch!" Justina yelped in agony while hopping back and forth on one leg.

I stopped dead in my tracks with the sole intention of blinding her with a twig. "'What in shite's name are you doing?" I snapped, feeling raw and frustrated.

She used her tongue to point at the foot that was in her hands. She had the splintered end of a large dry thorn sticking out of her instep. I berated her for running around barefoot; inside I was doing the happy dance for having second thoughts about ditching my Yoda slippers in the kitchen.

"Do something!" I shouted at Nick and Rufus, who was supposed to be a safety officer. They were completely useless standing side-by-side like poles with eyes. To make matters worse my first aid skills were submerged in my alcohol filled brain. All I could come up with was, "pull it out."

She yanked it out, and fell to the ground landing on her bum with a cushioned thud. She spent a good minute staring at the long thorn, with us gawking at her like witnesses to a car crash.

"Okay, the freak show is over," she snarled. All three of us jumped to help her to her feet, but Nick lost his footing and careened to the side felling down a row of saplings on his way.

"Great; now Koos has a valid reason to smother me in my bed," I moaned as he lay on the ground in a mangled mound of broken twigs and twisted limbs.

Rufus was aghast, "Jeez lady! Have you no sympathy?" he sounded like a belligerent child.

I stared into his sleepy left eye and replied, "no, but I'd appreciate you getting your colleague off those plants before Koos blows his head off with a sawn off .22."

Justina dusted the seat of her pyjamas and hobbled away, "let's get this over and done with: I need to get back to Abe before his conscience takes over his lustful urges," she announced to all and sundry. Rufus made a throaty sound while fretting over now upright Nick like an obsessive mother hen. The ungrateful egg brushed Rufus off making a beeline for Justina.

"Did you just say what I thought you were saying?" he asked tapping her on the shoulder to emphasise the urgency of his query.

She shrugged his hand off, "concentrate on your job and leave the voyeurism to Ricky Lake."

He slowed down so Rufus could catch up with him, and then then proceeded to give him a blow-by-blow account of his fantastic Friday night bender. I stifled the compulsion to laugh out loud at his ludicrous yarn. It ended with him tied down by two page three girls that had their way with him until Monday morning.

I wedged myself between them, "I hope they gave

you a frequent change of rubbers; I'd hate to see the state of your pickle if they didn't." The flicker of concern in his dark brown eyes made my stomach churn. "Why do you people insist on being another depressing statistic for the World Health Organisation?" I queried. Nick pounced on me for addressing him with a colonial tone. He demanded that I give an accurate description of the social grouping collectively known as "you people".

"It better be good because I've been trying to solve this riddle since the first time I was conscious of being patronised." He said.

I giggled heartily and replied, "I'm sorry Nick but you'd better get used to people being condescending, if you're going to run around in that black skin behaving like an aristocratic euro-trash brat in a Ferrari with no wheels. Frankly I'm sick of you upwardly-mobile types. You are so consumed by your possessions you forget your mortality in a dynamic universe with secrets that are deadlier than Syphilis and the HIV. You are reckless and drunk on the bogus supremacy points you gain as you move further away from the real values that add some meaning to everything you are."

He looked at me like I'd just swallowed a live asp, "you keep judging me like you know me; which I find very offensive by the way."

I made a general comment about the discomfort the truth can cause when it has it be swallowed whole.

"This bloody thing is locked," Justina growled

amidst the rustle of the chain she was trying to wrestle loose.

You could have knocked me over with a feather when I laid eyes on the heavy metal door with an electronic lock. The barn didn't even have hinges to hang a door on when Abe and I cleared out Wilma's rubbish a couple of weeks earlier. The junk was mostly aborted needlepoint and painting projects whose ugliness justified them being relegated to bonfire fuel. I shook the steel grate with all my might as the adrenalin rushed to my head, inflating my perception of my physical strength.

"What the bloody hell is going on around here? If this is another surprise from Eliza I'll kick her face in so hard; she won't be able to fit her fat imbecilic head into her wedding gown." I grumbled, and then yelped in agony when I somehow managed to sprain my left thumb. Once again Rufus and Nick were bemused beyond mobility, in the mean-time Justina and I displayed our familiarity with the universal book of curses.

Nick came back to his senses; "I can't work like this; call us when you've sorted yourself out, but bear in mind that these scheduled appointments are on the tax payers' tab." He said, making the most of his moment of self-righteousness now that our apparent lack of professionalism was in question.

"It's hardly her fault that some DIY lunatic is running amok on the estate," Justina spoke up in my defence, even though I'd side-tracked her from her new pursuit. I did the decent thing and invited them up to the hotel for refreshments while I figured out how to open the mysterious door. There was a sullen consensus, and then we trudged back to the house via the vegetable patch.

We were greeted by yet another melodramatic scene: Lucia was sobbing in Alana's arms at the far end of the table. Abe sat on the other end nibbling on dry toast.

"Can't you find something better to eat?" I asked him with the hope of detracting attention from the operatic melodrama that was unfolding.

"I'm fighting off nausea," he replied, pointing at Lucia, whom I assumed was the cause for his queasiness.

Alana had the sense to cart her off to her quarters to my relief. We could still hear their angry hisses and the occasional loud snivel, which was preferable to having to look at Lucia's scrunched-up face. I steamed some life into one day-old scones while Justina made a fresh pot of tea. Abe kept the reluctant company from making a break for it by indulging them with snapshots of his octane free life in Amish country. They seemed mildly amused by what they assumed was another kooky yarn cooked up by another one of my mentally unstable employees. Justina took the guests and the tea things to the conservatory, and I joined them for long enough to steal a spoonful of lemon and toasted poppy seed curd for my rice cake.

"I'm off to the barn," I announced as I rushed out to get Abe and the angle grinder. He was still seated at the kitchen table cradling his head in his hands like an old man that had truly seen it all.

"What's up stud muffin?" I greeted him as cheerily as I could.

"What do I have to fix this time?" he groaned miserably, rubbing his face with inappropriate vigour.

I ruffled his hair, "I have to find Koos and I need you to be my mouth piece. In exchange you can tell me why you are beating yourself up over a few orgasms."

He brushed my hand off his head. "I'll come with you if you promise to never ever stroke me like that. You make me feel like a cocker spaniel; it's kind of weird." He complained.
We scampered off when we heard an urgent shuffling of feet emanating from Alana's room. When we reached the edge of the orchard that he broke the comfortable silence.
"I like what happened between me and Justina. Lucia is a pain in my arse; she told me that I'm damaged goods now. It's how she said it that bothers me, t she thinks I'm diseased or something." He paused for a moment, scratching his head, "do you think Justina has STDs?" he asked.

My pace slackened, "tell me you used protection," I scolded him; feeling more subdued than I sounded.

He went scarlet, "I'm not really sure, but she did make me wear a ginseng and ginger flavoured rubber." His quivering chin kept me from falling over in hysterics. I took his hand in mine instead and assured him that scented condoms are excellent protection.

He brightened up, "I'm not completely naïve you know, I was just wondering if ninety-something percent safe is safe enough, and if she would tell me if there was something horribly wrong with her. Lucia says that nice girls don't stock up on condoms."

My blood simmered but I took pains to not let it go to my head; "nice girls have unprotected sex with their fingers crossed and they usually end up picking up nasty infections from equally idiotic men. If I were you I'd be patting myself on the back for picking the sensible easy lay over the psycho virgin. I'm really disappointed in you for winding yourself up over Lucia's mash of destructive bullshit, and sour grapes. She's just hurt because you were the closest she could get to her convent girl fantasy of getting down and dirty with Jesus Christ." He laughed then told me that I'd make a great father someday.

"I should probably let Lucia know that I do care for her even though I'm not the least bit attracted to her." He said.

I suggested that he advances with great caution since Lucia was still brooding over the way he had trampled on her sand castle and the sand people orgy inside it. As much as I didn't know the sordid details, I could still imagine how she might have felt hearing their grunts and moans from her room. The only way she could've been oblivious of the situation is if she'd been in a deep coma because her room shared a wall with Justina's.

Two hours later Abe and I were still standing outside the barn waiting for the locksmith's verdict while he fiddled and poked at the door. He threw his hands up in defeat and turned to us, "I'm sorry lady but I'm not a safe cracker. The only person that can open this door is the one that knows the bloody combination to that fucking lock," he spoke while packing his tools.

I already knew that Eliza had nothing to do with it which left Koos as the only other candidate that could've been responsible. But why would he invest his salary on costly security for an empty barn that didn't even belong to him? The useless locksmith ripped me off a hundred rand for his time and then he made the following suggestion, "you should call the police; you never know if someone is chopping cars in there."

I was fed up with him so I said, "Yeah, yeah, it could also be a secret freezer for cannibal burger meat suppliers. The fact remains that you're as ineffective as a pincushion in a bakery which is why you should fuck off before Abe takes my money back from you."

He shouted a bunch of expletives in Afrikaans as he headed back to his car which was parked a few yards away next to Koos' tractor.

"The next time you chuck me into the death ring at least make sure you pick an opponent that's not built like a chest-freezer on stilts." Abe

We kept a wary eye on the inadequate beast's car as it bounced down the valley on the dirt-road leading to the back gate. We both jumped out of our skins when Thomas spoke from behind us, "Where the hell is Koos?"
 We shrugged to express our ignorance regarding the racist horticulturist's whereabouts. He shook his head, "you must not let him go over your head when it comes to things like this," he grumbled pointing at the impenetrable door.

I nodded like an extra in a string puppet show, "I'm sick of people blaming me for everyone else's madness," I whined.

 His next swipe took Abe unawares; "I hear that you've been having trouble keeping the Amish stallion away from the fillies." He said.

Abe turned a yet unnamed shade of scarlet, "I take it you ran into the  village griot," he stammered, mortified by the prairie fire effect his erection had had on the local rumour factory. There was an uncomfortable silence accompanied by a lot of fidgeting from Abe's end.

"I would have gone for her too; the other one is complicated in a creepy sort of way." Thomas mused out loud. This time we all laughed. "Would it mean a lot to you if I somehow managed to open that door?" he asked me.

I had never come across what was in his eyes then, but I understood that if my mind had been steeped in religious hocus-pocus and supernatural crap then the middle-aged stranger would be my guardian angel. I didn't question him when he ordered us back to the house.

"What makes you think he's going to succeed where a proper locksmith failed," Abe asked me as soon as Thomas was out of sight.

"I don't really know, what I'd really like to know is why he keeps tools in his boot." I replied. That made him cackle like an old witch bent over a cauldron that's bubbling with the juices of Tinkerbelle and the tooth fairy.

"I'm not an expert on cars but I'm pretty sure that most motorists keep tools in their cars," he quipped with a generous helping of smarmy brat.

"Wrong again wagon boy; spanners and screwdrivers live in the boot, sophisticated safe-cracking tools do not live in your average family sedan."
He looked thoughtful for a moment, and then he diagnosed me with a fatal crush on Thomas.

"That makes me feel quite grubby, like you are accusing me of suppressing incestuous impulses." I replied.

He blushed, not realising that my cocky façade is just a shelter for the gnawing feeling that chance was not the only catalyst of my connection with Thomas.

"You will stir until I tell you to stop," the voice was unmistakably Alana's.
We quickened our pace expecting to find Justina chained to the stove; instead we happened upon Nick and Rufus out of their suit jackets. They were slaving over bubbling pots of citrus smelling gooey stuff with their shirtsleeves rolled up to their armpits. The misery on their faces was sweeter than the sight of them making jam.

"She caught them eating her curdle," Lucia explained perkily. She looked a sight better with a fresh layer of make-up over her tear streaked cheeks.

"So you've finally swallowed those sour grapes then?" I pointed out thoughtlessly.

Abe sprang to her side in a desperate attempt to win her over with a feeble act of chivalry but ended up bearing the brunt of her wrath.

"'I don't need your pity mister wandering snake," she spat.

He got the hint and turned his attentions to Alana's conscripts opting for watching rather than lifting a finger to ease their plight. They were uncharacteristically pliable under her iron fist; not even a peep came out of them as they tended the simmering jam.

"This is totally out of order, you should know better

than to treat government officials like colonial slaves." I ranted at Alana.

She blanched, "to me they are just children that helped themselves to an extra bottle of curdle. Deal with your prejudices!"

The civil servants kept on stirring as if abiding by Alana was the most natural thing in the world. I remembered what Jamie would say to console me when Jessie became too overbearing, "in Africa you remain a child for as long as there is an older person around to put you in your place." Despite how little I thought of Nick I could at least respect his ability to express humility when it was absolutely necessary to do so.

"That's enough my lieflings," Alana said after sampling both bubbling pots of jam. "I'll fix us some nice ginger beer and coconut cookies," she beamed at them, glowing with pride.

"Get a hold of yourself woman, they're just a pair of jam stirring twits. It's not like they've made gold from ether," Lucia sniped at her new ally.

**Chapter 7**

Thomas burst in clearly shaken, "did you know that you've got a barn full of fertiliser and Sodium-Peroxide?" he glowered at me and then cast a suspicious glance in Alana's direction. I shook my head in slow motion- partly because my mind was moving too fast in directions I'm still not entirely comfortable with. I must have looked a confused mess on the outside because Thomas emphasised every syllable when he said, "do you understand what that implies?"

I nodded, "I know more about bombs than your average terrorist," I said more to myself than anyone else. I wished I'd said nothing when I turned to Nick and Rufus who were seated at the table looking like they needed sugary water.

Rufus suddenly came to life with authoritative force, "from what I know about homemade explosives; I can tell you now that this is no small matter," he observed.

The news went down like a bombshell to everyone else but Thomas and me. Horror was expressed in several different languages but Nick's vacant "fuck me!" took the cake.

"I'm calling the police," Rufus declared with finality.

"I'm not hanging around for the boys in ill-fitting blue uniforms," Thomas stated flatly.

Rufus' vehement protest against him leaving merely caused more commotion but achieved nothing. "You better start thinking of a good explanation for how you single-handedly worked your way around breaking the code for that complicated locking device," he told me.

"Hold on a second; I'm more the victim here than any of you oafs and here you are happily plotting the quickest way to chuck me in the deep-end." I exploded close enough to his face for his flared nostrils to singe my eyebrows.

He was even more annoyed than he was a few minutes earlier when Thomas threw him out of the way like a tattered rag doll that should've stayed at the bottom of the toy chest. Keen to reassert his flagging authority Rufus drummed on accusingly, "you were quite happy to let your dubious taxi driver friend take off, even though he seems to be an explosives expert with obviously unparalleled cat-burglary skills."

My bladder welled up as if to substantiate that Rufus had taken that round with a technical knockout.

Lucia harrumphed, "get over yourself Sherlock, for all you know Thomas has yanked your chain right off and you are standing here handing out punishment slips over something you haven't even seen for yourself. Once everyone's eyes were on her she grasped the opportunity to give Rufus "the finger". She emphasised her malicious intentions by jabbing the air with her digit while making barnyard noises. Her antics added an apocalyptic element to the melodrama; which unsettled me even more.

Alana swooped on her from nowhere like a ravenous fruit bat and thwacked her head so hard it bobbed about like a helium balloon on a string.

"Everyone to the barn," she shouted us off our chairs as effectively as a Hitler Jorgen squad leader.

True to Thomas' word the barn was a pyromaniac's dream come true. Nick made yet another comment that suggested a two digit IQ; "It looks like someone's planning to blow the whole world up." He was a picture of childlike animation as he hopped about trying to tot up the exact quantity of the five feet high, carefully stacked rows of twenty-five kilos fertiliser bags. I on the other hand felt another spell coming on from just looking at the vast quantities of benign looking five litre plastic bottles.

Then the entire police force materialised from ether as a storm of red dust, blue flashing lights, and a deafening cacophony of emergency sirens.

We awaited our fate helplessly as heavily armed men leapt out of various modes of armoured peacekeeping transportation. Their big guns were cocked and ready to fire as they encircled us. A cold hand gripped my arm just below the elbow, "I don't think I can take much more of this," Abe's voice quivered into my buzz-filled ear.

"Pull yourself together..." I started to speak but I was cut off by a policeman with a megaphone for a voice box.

"Put your hands up and move away from each other," he barked at us, making us leap in various directions.

Lucia shrieked in disgust from beneath Abe. Gravity had coerced him into reluctantly fulfilling a fraction of Lucia's aborted desire. Rufus stepped up and declared his status in the bureaucratic food-chain in a loud shaky voice, thus saving us from unnecessary torture by further humiliation. The battalion approached with less caution, which means that some of them tackled us to the ground and frisked the shit out of us while the others had their guns trained on our extremities.

"This is police brutality," I pointed out after spitting out much of the dust I had swallowed when I was romancing the ground.

"You people and your rights are getting right up my bum," the SWAT commander sneered.

He shoved me aside and then claimed that he had merely nudged me out of the way when I complained. I trailed after him, hopping mad at the way he'd handled me like a sack of unwashed potatoes.

"I will complain to your superiors about your storm trooper tactics." I said.

Mine was a lonely voice; the others were still readjusting the shit in the seats of their pants. Abe grabbed me by the scruff of my neck and told me to calm down before people got shot.

"It's not 1984 and I'm the victim in this ludicrous scenario," I complained. I suspended my tears for a private moment. "I'm going back to the house."

Another fray erupted when the others followed me leaving it up to an exasperated Rufus to be the barrier between us and the charging troops. He was about to be pounced on for the second time in two minutes when the commander ordered his troops to stand down.

"Let them go, but make sure that no one leaves the house," he said.

Rufus and Abe stayed behind to witness the search. Alana's khaki outfit looked three shades darker against her skin, which was drained of colour from head to toe.

"These Nazi fuckers are worse than the terrorists they claim to be fighting," she proclaimed once we were relatively safe behind the double-bolted kitchen door.

Justina crept out of Alana's room looking like a frightened African asylum-seeker in a Greek port. "What's going on out there?" she stage whispered slithering across the kitchen floor like a stumpy anaconda. "I was sleeping on that gazebo thing out there, and then this terrible noise woke me up. When I open my eyes I find some soldiers pointing all these guns at my face. I was afraid so I explained that I just make the beds. They asked for directions to the barn and told me to stay inside; what the hell is going on here?" She rested on her bottom to replenish her depleted stock of oxygen.

We took turns in elaborating on the emotional and violent content of the dark times we had in the hands of the law. She didn't care about the armoured cars, the guns or the helicopter on the lawn.

"Has anyone seen Koos?" she asked the unanswered question that each one of us had pondered during the various stages of the unfolding mystery.

Lucia gave her a wan smile, "that's the million dollar question darling," she replied, gesturing for her to come sit next to her. "I'll make us some tea. And you should get your bum off the floor before you get nasty haemorrhoids," she added while helping Justina up to her feet.

At that instant Lucia was as beautiful and as innocent as an alluvial diamond in the hands of a child. Her unexpected kindness after the acrimony from earlier on was a comforting indicator of progress in inter-personal relations. It was proof that we had evolved from a bunch of strangers trying to get along into a highly dysfunctional family with no fixed head.

"I guess twenty-two years of marriage does not qualify anyone to claim that they know everything there is to know about their spouse," Alana spoke so softly her words could have slipped under the table unnoticed.

Justina's hot mug of unsweetened tea froze midway to her mouth. "What are you talking about Alana?" she asked with a hint of discomfort.

Alana had the look of someone that had just awoken

from an action-packed dream when she recited a chapter of her life story. When she told us her story her voice had the same monotonous rhythm she employed when pounding sour-dough bread:

"Not that it's any of your business, but Koos and I were married for longer than most people's lifespan. This racist terrorist is not the man I left for not telling me the truth. He admitted that he was seeing someone but he wouldn't tell me who she was. He's always been a strange one; disappearing for days on end with no explanation and not a single apology. Besides that he was the perfect husband, until I ended it because I could no longer live with not knowing." She, made a face, and scrambled to her feet. "I better put the kettle on while you lot are playing dead," she told us off before disappearing into the larder.

"No offence, but you people need to have your heads checked." Nick gave his rude advice with a sneer.

Alana came out of the pantry with a basket. It contained: one fruit loaf, a jar of brandy and raisin sauce, two jars of pickled fish, three boxes of oatcakes, hot mango chutney, and two tubs of fresh cream.

 "Do I have to be crushed to death by these things to get help?" she moaned even though Justina was already on her feet.

"See what I mean, you should be locked up if you ask me," Nick teetered like a stoned cheerleader.

"Well, no one asked for your opinion," we roared in unison.

Our united voice made him fly off his chair and land on his back on the cold stone floor with a priceless look of shock and gut-flushing fear on his botoxed face. Well at least I thought it was; not once did I see a crease of emotion on his freakishly immobile skin.

We were on our second pot of tea after scoffing every scrap of Alana's pungent buffet; when Abe dragged himself through the open door looking like a ghost from the battle of Gettysburg. His lover was on her tip-toes in a flash planting kisses on his sun baked face and neck, "we were so worried about you." She cooed.

He wrinkled his freckled nose, "I think my stomach is eating itself." He said, holding her at arm's length.

She let go and turned away from him, "Sit down, I'll make you something to eat." She murmured. She shuffled off to the pantry looking like a giant fly that had just been swotted with the butt of a submachine gun.

Lucia followed her into the pantry and slammed the door shut but her piercing voice carried over to us. "It's not you; it's just that your breath is a bit rank at the moment, not that mine is any better," she bleated honestly.

Unfortunately Justina had developed selective deafness due to Abe's unintentional display of tactlessness. "The Atkinson's joke is played out, don't you think?"

"I was referring to the food we've just eaten, not your halitosis," Lucia shrieked
Her cheeks were red when she came out of the food closet.
She dished out curses in Spanish and Creole, "talk about stroking a poisonous snake." She said.

We responded with vague gestures that summed up to; "we heard every single word including the foreign bits, but we are not inclined to admit we'd been listening." Alana tugged at Abe's sleeve, "So, did they search all your orifices?" she cackled. Justina and Rufus started bickering about who had been traumatised the most. Lucia and Nick jumped into the fray with their own inventories of the psychological damages they had incurred that morning. It was at that point it occurred to me that I could seek sanctuary in the conservatory and not be mowed down by a hail of bullets on the way there.

Rufus threw cold water over my plan by turning up with the chief storm trooper who announced that I was to follow him, and the person stationed in the reception while they searched the hotel. I led the way cursing him under my breath for having the nerve to install a guard in the house without saying so.

"Arsehole," I cursed loud enough for him to hear me.

"I've been called worse, but I'm tempted to arrest you for that," he replied.

He pushed past me to brief his man, who was

lounging on a two-seater couch nursing a tumbler of what I hoped was cola. The expression on the commander's face confirmed otherwise, but I moved closer to have a sniff for myself anyway.

"Have you been stealing my booze?" I snarled at the cop. He stood up still clutching the offending cocktail of whisky, cola and brandy.

The commander went berserk, "You're useless man, even a teetotal retard knows that the only sensible thing to drink when on duty is vodka; plain and simple, unless you're a certified moron, which seem to be the norm in the police force these days." He turned to address me, "I've witnessed more incompetence in the last six years than I have in my thirty-six years of service."

I informed him that I preferred the inept drunks to the trigger-happy proficient racists from the old days. He instructed me to lead the way upstairs. "What do you expect to find?" I queried defensively, trudging up the stairs with him hot on my heels. They eventually left after searching every closet, drawer, and container on the property; they even dug up "suspicious" looking portions of the fallow fields.

Despite being weary and smelly, we all stayed in Alana's room until sometime after midnight. By then it was clear that none of us was brave enough to take the walk down the gravel path in case someone was lurking behind the bushes. Soon after that we started arguing over who would go on what bed. We had commandeered the family suite. Justina and Abe would have preferred to cuddle in the double bed, but Lucia was having none of it. "I'm not going to spend another night listening to your disgusting noises," she said.

The two Abe and Alana shared the bunk bed in the next room, Lucia took the single bed, and Justina slept with me in the master bedroom.

**Chapter 8**

There were literally dozens of e-mails from my aunt and all of them had the same subject matter. After going through several, I realised that they were all identical down to the barely legible yellow font. That was slightly disturbing; the fact that she didn't even mention the vomit incident also gave me the willies.

"My dearest Ceillidh

You'll never know how relieved I am to see how you've bloomed in spite of everything you went through so early in your life. I'm sorry I couldn't give straight answers to most of your questions. I hope you understand that it's because Thomas gave me very little warning. I'm not one for surprises of any sort. I'm sure you are less concerned about my habits so I'll get to the point.

I need your help in reigning Eve in; she's headed for a major knock but she's not aware of it because it's coming in small pretty boxes. She thinks her looks are a first class ticket to the hollow glamorous life she craves. Sometimes I think I should have enrolled her in a state-run, township school instead of me spending hundreds of thousands of rand on her schooling. All the money I've spent on her is wasted on her chasing mirages alongside kids that don't have limited alternatives. She doesn't realise how lucky she is to have all that she has, or that it's important that she use her disadvantage to better herself.

My only child thinks I'm certifiably mad, because I can't bear to see her turn into a drone. Thomas will bring her to you on Friday; I hope you'll have talked some sense into her head come Sunday. As for me, everything that comes out of my mouth sounds loopy to her. There's not much of a chance that I'll make a difference at all. Please don't try to call me. I'd prefer to communicate this way until I get back to my usual self. I will not pick up the phone under any circumstances!

Your loving aunt

Rosemary"

I dialled her number over and over again only to get through to an electronic voice with a pornographic timbre urging me to leave a message. My face sunk into my hands, tears streaming through the cracks between my trembling fingers. I squeezed my eyes shut until I felt nothing but the warmth of the red glow in the dark.

"Dear Aunt Rosemary
What the hell do you expect me to do with all this? Much as I appreciate your state of mind, I will not accept your decision to avoid talking. I want to know why you rejected me and ejected me to Scotland like an orphaned refugee. You knew my mother just before she had me. You must have known she was pregnant; after all you two were very "close". I'm also aware that you'll still send Eve over for the weekend despite the fact that you've peed on the novelty of me getting in touch with my roots. So tell Eve that I'm looking forward to seeing her. As for you, you can fester in the past with your miserable ghosts for all I care.

Yours sincerely

Ceillidh"

The door swung open, and Abe stepped aside to reveal a heavily decorated middle-aged, black police officer. He looked more like a successful banker than an award winning crime stopper. He strode over to me smiling broadly, and introduced himself as superintendent Mokoena.

"I apologise for popping in unannounced; but there's no other option considering the circumstances." He said.

I nodded, temporarily dumbfounded by his enchanting smile, which made me grin like an idiot on happy pills. He perched beside me on the window seat. "Do you have any idea where Mr Koos Malherbe could be, or who he's most likely to contact?" I laughed aloud at his question giving him a clear view of my epiglottis. "I wasn't aware of my comic talents Ms McLaughlin," he replied; leaving me with the discomfiting notion that I'd hurt the nice man's feelings unnecessarily.

"I'm sorry sir, it's just that Koos and I have hardly said a word to each other since I arrived here, he's a bit of a racist." I replied truthfully.

"Yet you still kept him as your gardener?' he probed as the kindly veneer slipped to reveal the calculating streak that had earned him his stars. I shrunk away from him involuntarily.

"Is there anything else I can do for you other than capturing Koos and handing him over to you that is?" I responded with a well-practised snarl that usually sends veteran thugs running for cover.

"I'll be in touch." He stated flatly, sullying my mental record of his impeccable manners by swaggering away without a word of leave.

"He could have waited for me to walk him to the front door," Abe complained as he shut the door firmly behind him. "Besides that man, what else is eating you?" he asked. I tried to smile and fob him off with a breezy response but nothing sprung to mind. His eyes were oozing the warmth I desperately needed so I just let go. He held me tight saying, "there, there," while I sobbed my heart out for a good fifteen minutes. "Are you sure you don't want to talk about it?" he asked for the hundredth. I disentangled myself from him out of propriety, when all I really wanted to do was to remain cocooned until the truth faded into the background. I put on a bright smile and soldiered on.

"Don't mind me I'm just experimenting with vulnerability." I said.

He laughed and then we linked arms and walked to the kitchen. "Justina's made six different vegetarian quiches," he told me as we strolled down the hallway.

I made the ravenous sounds that Jamie would use as his irreverent way of saying grace for Jessica's tenderly assembled meals. The crack of a smile on Abe's sunburnt face reassured me that the deception was complete. It took the sting out of slipping into my together persona as I took my place at the head of the table.

"Do you want salad, or grilled vegetables?" Justina asked as I tried to swallow an outsized forkful of soggy cardboard.

It could have been the tastiest quiche my tongue had ever encountered, but I had too much on my mind.

"I'll try both," I said with false gusto.

I might have fooled the younger ones with my phantom appetite and upbeat demeanour, but Alana was familiar with the symptoms of suppressed emotions. "You'll help me pick some berries later," she told me.

"Why should I go picking berries? I have tons to do before Friday?" I replied with a crack of exasperation in my gratingly chirpy voice.

She held me down with an icy glare, "I have to make tons of cheesecake for the stupid wedding, and I'm not taking one of the girls because they have lots of scrubbing and polishing to do today." I nodded, but only because I had none of the energy required to do a battle of wills with a veteran of wars I'd never even heard of.

"I don't think that policeman believed a word you said to him," Lucia was addressing Alana. "Then again it does seem implausible that while we were sleeping like logs; the gardener was preparing for a major terrorist attack," she concluded pensively.

Abe banged his head against the table top; sending cutlery and crockery flying in all directions. The rest of us scrambled around the room saving plates and side plates from certain destruction. We looked on in awe as he ranted, "If you could just coax your heads out of your arseholes for a moment, you might realise that none of us have a clue about what Koos gets up to day or night. We are in no position to make any judgements. For all we know; the poor old man could be in a shallow grave under any one of those saplings in the orchard."

A wave of chills spread around the table like an aggressive cancer that feeds on nightmares. Abe lurched towards the door just as Justina reached out to him, leaving her arm dangling mid-air like the remnants of a derelict signpost in a ghost town. Alana smiled at her malevolently, "you've really outdone yourself." She told the stricken girl who was trying not to blink so her curtain of tears wouldn't fall along with her resolve to conceal the intensity of the sharp pain in her gut. I took my plate to the sink avoiding Lucia's roving gaze.

"'Can we go now please; I've got tons to do." I grumbled on my way to the door. Hard graft under the glaring sun suddenly seemed like my lucky dip ticket out of kitchen sink dramas and desolation.

"Sometimes the decent thing to do is to act like you care; these kids are as far away from home as they'll ever be and it's our duty to be grown up when they need to be children." Alana scolded me as we walked side by side on the gravelled path.

I was too busy relishing the life affirming sensation of my skin baking under the sun I forgot to respond.

"Are you going to tell me what's going on, or will I have to use my divining bones to work this one out?" she grilled me. She adamantly picked at the bone that had already been chewed dry by a family of grizzlies on a budget vacation in the Serengeti.

I told her the entire tale of my worries in one long sentence punctuated with a sigh and a shriek rose up from my belly; it shook all the milk tarts in every home industry store and every baking oven in Parys. "I'm okay now," I said. I was slightly embarrassed, but liberated of the niggling feeling that I was about to explode. I realised that it would be a while before Alana would be able to say anything; her face had turned a pale shade of blue. She was still able to walk only because her feet had stopped listening to her head. The stillness seemed to amplify the slow crunch of our footsteps accompanied by the buzz of insects going about their everyday tasks of pillaging, sheltering, and nurturing in their vibrant kingdom of deep green foliage and bold colours.
The wedding

We spent all morning making sure that Magdalene finds nothing to deride, one of her infamous hissy-fits would be enough to turn us into a bloodthirsty pack of hyenas on a moonless night.
Megan, the trendy features writer arrived after dinner on the eve of Eliza's wedding day; she turned out to

be as likeable as a mature boil on the bum. In fact she nearly drove us to the mental asylum with her impossible demands, and generally taking the piss at the energy we put into her comfort. Her male bauble was mortified beyond speech throughout the gruesome ordeal. He didn't look a day over nineteen; his wear-worn baggy jeans made that assumption more of a fact. It was probably due to him that I finally cracked when she sent me out to pick her a sprig of mint at 3am. She felt that the batch that Alana had picked earlier in the day was not fresh enough to go into her Pimms and lemonade. I had a private chat with the others, and we decided that we'd taken enough nonsense from a borderline paedophile to last us several doggy lifetimes.

She looked like she'd been slapped on the face with a five-pound tuna when Alana said, "You may spend the night, considering that you're too pissed to drive back to Joburg with a twelve-year old. As for the boy, he sleeps in the family room with Abe. I'm not risking charges for aiding and abetting a statutory rapist."

First she tried indignation, and then she dished out threats. She eventually gave in when she tried to unlock the railway sleeper door with her car key. I assured her that everything that went on in all the public areas was recorded on CCTV just in case vitriol spurred her into dreaming up a caustic write-up. None of us got the chance to speak to her in the morning because she bolted from the stable without rousing her young stallion.

"I'll help out with the wedding for my bus fare," the stranded lad bargained, when the local girl that I had enlisted for extra help decided not to turn up.

"Look kiddo, that's very enterprising of you; but I'm not going to let a teenager gagging on his silver spoon and ruined the most important day in that annoying girl's dull life." Alana replied, before I'd had a chance to consider Uri's tempting proposition.

He ignored her and addressed me instead, which isn't much of a feat if you're slightly over three-foot-nine. I stared at him vacuously, "I've been working in my parents' Steers restaurant since I was twelve; I'm a very good worker," he said. I was impressed, bearing in mind that his eyes were a few blinks away from raising the floodgates. I remained outwardly impassive despite the: tongue wagging, cheek jiggling, happy face party that was in full swing just beneath my skin.

"You stay here, and do anything Alana tells you to do as fast and efficiently as humanly possible." I told him after a calculated overlong period of stillness and left the room. I avoided a nasty collision with the wedding cake when I stumbled on the toes of a tattooed sailor who was built like the rock beneath the temple of the mount.

"Watch where you're going Ms Chaka Kahn," he jibed unwisely at the state of my heat-frizzed hair. I brushed off the impulse to shove his face into the disconcertingly accurate kissing profiles of the bride and groom nestling at the centre of the red, heart-shaped cake he was carrying. It was probably created by the ghost of a master artist whose spirit was trapped in an empty oilcan under the false bottom of Magdalene's DIY cosmetic surgery toolkit.

"Good morning gentlemen. Alana should be in the kitchen; she'll sort you right out." I murmured as I negotiated my way past the last of the mincing entourage and their load of "fabulous" crap. I had to blink a dozen times for my brain to compute that Magdalene and an unknown man were in the café directing a team that was covering my lovely new seats with African print throws. She was giving the place a quick makeover with what seemed like a truckload of stuff I'd never laid my eyes on in all my days. I could not find the words to express my anger, so I went on a destructive rampage ripping and smashing any alien object I could get my hands on. I had to dodge and duck an army of limbs whose sole intent was to bring me down to the ground. The multi-limbed beast finally caught up with me, wedging me between the legs of a Victorian settee and the base of a translucent egg chair.

"Let me go!" I yelled with the last breath of air that had not been knocked out of me.

Magdalene's white snakeskin pumps were the last thing I saw before a volatile vomit attack struck me. It brought me pretty close to inhaling a healthy lungful of a stodgy puree with an unpleasant smell and kaleidoscopic qualities. Magdalene's pointy shoe missed my nose by a hair as she took off on her hop around the room, trying to shake my incredibly adhesive puke off her shoe. I helped myself up since all her minions were rallying around her as if she were a victim of a drive-by shooting. "They are vintage Kurt Geiger's," her second in command moaned as he crouched to assess the damage on Magdalene's sodden left shoe. He sprung nimbly to his feet, "well at least that one got away with a few splatters. I've got this friend, Cedric, he owns a valet service. He works miracles on a daily basis." He said brightly.

I moistened my throat with rancid saliva, "magic yourself, your shit, and your entourage out of here before I blow my entire fuse box." I said.

Magdalene almost snapped her neck spinning around to face me; the intensity of her steely gaze forced me to leap onto the table. I was afraid it would become absolutely necessary for one of us to die from one swift blow on the head struck from above; my hitting hand automatically clenched into a manly fist.

"My, what big hands you have," said the cake bearing sailor from earlier on.

The mob that seemed to have orbed from the kitchen turned the reception into a cinema foyer on the premiere night of a blockbuster film. Alana burst her way through the throng of bodies to take her rightful place on the table beside me. "You have another thing coming if you think you can just drop in with your *pink* army and declare yourself dictator of the manor." She spat, jabbing a finger too close to Magdalene's eye. She looked like an incensed troll with murder on her mind. Lucia and Justina also sprung to action clearing the room of the jungle of accessories.

"You can't just throw my things outside like that," Felipe protested to no avail. Crash went what turned out to be a set of leopard print crystal glasses in a customised wooden case.

"You should have put a "fragile" sticker on it." Justina pointed out while dunking the last bunch of exotic grasses into Felipe's box of broken treasures.

He looked up from inspecting the wreckage and snapped. "I can't believe you just did that," he cried out, stretching to his full height in a single panther like movement. Justina stood her ground daring him to make the first the move. "I'd kick the rainbow into your arse if you had balls," he sneered. I believed him; he was built like a boxer.

"If you don't excuse yourself from the wedding you can take your money back and book an entire campsite. That way you can make the most of your jungle theme; you can even build a fire if you want." I whispered into Magdalene's twitching ear. She was standing beside me on the doorstep devouring Felipe's forearms with her permanently startled eyes.

"Your breath stinks like Crème de menthe and vomit," she shrunk back in disgust.

"I had to wash the puke down with something." I replied. "So are you staying, or is the wedding going?" We glared at each other with the intensity of punch drunk veteran street fighters conceding to a draw, secretly savouring the sight of each other's open wounds.

She left me alone on the step, "I'm off to the spa for a long luxurious afternoon of pampering and disinfection." she tossed the words over her shoulder along with her exquisite sliver of a pale yellow silk scarf. Her bony pianist's fingers stroked Felipe's back as she murmured platitudes into his ear, gently coaxing him away from the fray. Time stood still as we followed their slow progress towards his gleaming beast of a convertible Jaguar. I was literally counting down their last three steps when the wedding convoy pulled into the driveway in true carnival spirit. The sun shone brighter because of the stream of cars that poured in dressed in balloons and streamers that were dancing in the spring breeze to the tooting horns. I couldn't muster the venom to carry out Magdalene's banishment.

"Come back you crazy old tart," I pleaded breathlessly after doing a ninety meters sprint in eight seconds flat.

"I'll do it for Timothy," she agreed huffily.

I had a feeling that the thought of her husband loathing her more than he already did made her rethink her afternoon of credit card busting inertia. Felipe drove off in an angry cloud of gravel.

"There should be a law against selling such a beautiful machine to a complete idiot," Paul sneered in disgust. He walked towards his wife, his mind clearly rifling through a molehill of wholesome explanations for her presence.

"I thought I'd surprise both families with a little

something, but it all went pear-shaped as you can see," she explained before he could air his confusion. She used her arms as a pointer with the flair of a seasoned shopping channel presenter. Not once did she moan about her sick sodden shoe when she began fussing with Paul's bowtie; he was bemused beyond speech.

Eliza trudged towards us clutching her bouquet in one hand and the hem of her skirt in the other. "You didn't have to do that," she said, tears streaming down her face. I cast a glance at Felipe's band of merry workers as they retreated into their pink Hummer leaving debris of shattered glass and twigs in their wake.

"You are better off bawling at your mother in law if you're after a proper explanation. As for me, I'm just here for the ride." I replied, with one eye trained on the ludicrously large truck as if that would keep it from flattening Koos' neat edges.

"I'm talking about the bandstand," she interrupted my thoughts with a wobbly whine. "It's beautiful.'

A mighty force spun me around to face Eliza. "Oh," I replied with a slack- jawed, owlish expression.

**Chapter 9**

The sun had worked up the stomach to turn her face away from the wonder that is Africa, and we were more than willing to do the same after seeing the backs of the buoyant wedding party. "That went too smoothly if you ask me." Lucia observed ominously. We were strewn around the conservatory like partially deflated rubber dolls- surrounded by platters of equally unappealing remnants of our buffet.

"There's a car coming up the driveway," said someone. Lucia and I raced to the window on all fours. Sure enough there was a set of headlights creeping up on the manor.

"Great, here come a couple of overnighters we cannot afford to turn away." I complained as two figures emerged from a mini. Alana let out an operatic sigh, which had Abe and Justina in stitches. "Shit, shit, shit." I proclaimed, furiously padding towards the door on the palm of my hands leaving a noisy trail of spare change on the hardwood floor. I turned the doorknob with my toes then pushed the door open without crippling any major muscle groups.
The people in the mini turned out to be Eve, and a boy called Gavin. They joined us as we picked at the leftovers of our leftovers. We told them about our day, and they told us everything about their drive; not a peep as to why they had bothered coming that far in the first place.

"Your mum said you'd be over next weekend..." my words trailed off when I noticed the tears streaming down her face. "I'm sorry," I said. My words came out like a question instead of a consolatory gesture, which made me rue the day I was blessed with a mouth.

"Sometimes I feel like no one cares," she sniffled, and then rushed out of the room with Gavin hot on her heels. "This is not happening," I started muttering the mantra just under my breath as I followed my troubled visitors. I heard Alana volunteering to fetch some brandy.

"I just don't want it to end like this," Gavin stage whispered from an unlit corner of the reception area. I was contemplating quietly scuttling away from what seemed like a regular break-up, but Alana wouldn't let me.
We crept so expertly; I could've sworn that we teleported ourselves behind the bar. We stayed beneath the counter, eavesdropping over a half-empty bottle of martini. "I'm just not ready to stop, not now anyway, okay?" she paused as if to balance herself for the blow she was about to deliver. "I'm not the same girl that used to tag along on your family outings just to catch a bit of sunshine."

"I'm sorry, but I don't know what you're talking about. I didn't realise that's how you felt." He sounded as if he was unsure of how he might have precipitated her sudden breakdown.

"Then why do you stay in the car every time you come to my house? Why don't we ever talk about my life in the cling filmed bubble?" she paused to draw breath. "I'm sick of watching you trying to save me by pretending my life is normal." She sounded cold; her words chilled me despite the warm fluid going down my throat.

"You just want to fuck the Nigerian dude. Go ahead I know when my game is up." He said. I started choking, and then I heard door slamming and the car screeching out of the driveway five minutes later. It was two days later and once again I stood outside her door with a tray of food and the day's papers. I knew that she was awake because I could hear her rearranging the furniture for the hundredth time.

"Here's your food and papers," I shouted at the door: No answer. "If you're not ready to come out in two hours; I'll ask Thomas to fetch your mother," I added before returning to my prison on the stoep. I was starting to lose my grip on reality. I had been keeping watch over her since she retreated into my spare room; Alana wouldn't let her sleep in the hotel.

"I think she might do something stupid. Look at her; she's practically chewing her face from the inside out." She'd said in defence of her decision. I didn't know where to begin explaining that Eve was *pilled* out of her funny mind.

"Just get me a fucking joint," Eve spoke through the door for the first time since she had opted for self-imposed solitude. Justina was on my doorstep with a bag of greens exactly five minutes after I'd put down the phone. She rolled a ridiculously long joint with one of the meter-long rolls of hemp papers she kept in her underwear drawer.

"Rooibos, or Chamomile tea?" I yelled from the kitchen.

"Does it matter?" Eve replied.

I rolled my eyes to the heavens, cursing my aunt for saddling me with a casualty of matters of the heart. I had enough on my serving platter as it were.

Eve emerged from the bedroom looking like a bowling alley pin from hell "Are you going to light that?" she said. "Thanks but I don't drink herbal tea." She pushed the mug away.

"You're welcome," I replied. Justina cast me a furtive glance from across the table before passing the joint to Eve. I shrugged and turned my attention to the stream.

"You don't have to look away, it's not like I'm sucking on a crack pipe." She objected.

"Are you a crack-head? In case I do give a rat's arse." I replied without looking at her. I had to restrain myself from the urge to pour hot tea down her nostrils. She waved the joint into my line of vision and I grabbed it as rudely as it was offered to me.

"I can't do crack; I'd like it too much,' she replied.

"Come again?" Justina managed to say in a small voice.

My mouth remained agape for a good minute: it was

physically impossible for me to move a single muscle. Eve glared into my vacant eyes. "You and I need to get out of here as soon as the day before you landed on my mother's front door." She said. Now that had me freaking out. I fished for one of the trillions of questions that were swimming in my head- but all I came out with was a pathetic, "why me?" I didn't appreciate what Justina was insinuating by that chortle, and I was going to tell her as soon as I could get my hands around her neck someplace private.

"Should we go inside?" I emphasized the urgency to be inside with hand gestures. Justina chuckled.

"Do you think the monsters from your cousin's deep-fried brain are lurking in the foliage?" She teased.

"Your day off might come to an abrupt end." I said, trying to extricate myself from the rocking chair without dropping the joint into the mug.

"You should've passed that thing before dunking it in your tea," Eve started complaining, but gave up when no one minded her. "You and I need to make some life and death decisions real quick." she said, once we were in the living room.

Justina leapt to her feet, "maybe I should give you guys some space." She said.

I shook my head vigorously; I did not want her to leave me alone with my cousin's psychotic episode.

"Let her go please." Eve's plea super-sized the lump

in my throat.

I only nodded in agreement because I could no longer breathe. The treacherous Justina was out the door before I could blink away my tears of fear. "What's this about then?" I put on a brave front but inside I was a confused quivering mess of jelly.

She was in no hurry to give answers, "let me finish rolling this." she said, and then proceeded to exhibit the dexterity of her elegant digits. I recollected my jumbled up thoughts under the pretext of getting juice and vegetable crisps.

She said, "I still think it will be better for everyone if we get the hell out of here." She nibbled on a pumpkin crisp; "I've got my passport here with me. I always have it with me. You never know where the night will take you."

"I could hit you with a blunt object over your head and throw you into the stream. That way you'll never have to deal with me, your mother, and the long list of crazies that are out to get you." I said. I did not have to look at her to see the effect of my flippant comment. I waited for her to stop choking on pot smoke and veggie bits wondering if her mother was aware of how dangerously fucked-up her woman-child had become.

She wiped the dribble off her chin, "I'm sorry; but not all of this mess is my fault."

"Just get on with it, will you?" I drilled into her persistently.

She sighed, "I met this Zambian guy called Sammy at Micky's party on Saturday. He had enough *blow* to keep an army marching for days, so he invited me and Gav to chill with him. The next thing I know I'm on my way here in a strange car," she paused to take a deep drag, and then she blew out a colossal coil of smoke that snaked its way over our heads and turned into nothing.

According to Eve her friend Micky's party was like Ibiza in the heat of summer. There were dozens of cosy nooks for new found lovers to canoodle in, and crannies for soulless drug sluts to flash their tits for limitless lines of cocaine and frenetic sex with men that have lost all sensation. The mansion was that weekend's shrine for the serious party crowd, and the seriously lost degenerates that crept out at night to feed their personal sewers. She was familiar with almost everyone that was at that party; they had been a permanent fixture in her life for the four years she had been best-friends with Michaela.

She and Michaela had been natural enemies from the instant they met on their first day of high school. That is the reason why they were both shaken when they found themselves in the same trench against a common foe. That was in the tenth grade, and their mutual enemy was their science teacher, Mr Bell.

They always found excuses for spending half his class in their favourite cubicles in the girl's loo. Eventually Mr Bell got fed up enough to burst into the toilets and confiscate their packs of cigarettes. Marching them to the principal's office was the worst decision of his teaching career; the situation ended badly for him because they wrongfully accused him of sexual harassment and got away with the deception. They claimed that it was discomfort that had made them keep away from his class. The country was already in the grips of paedophilia-hysteria, which helped drive the headmistress to the conclusion that Mr Bellman had framed them to silence them. It wasn't easy for them to see him drowning in the pool of fabricated sleaze as more "cases" crawled out of the woodwork. At the time his fall from grace was far more preferable to living with the diminished trust and judgement that would surely be in their parents' eyes had they confessed to smoking.

The weight of the lie drew them closer to each other, and the guilt dissipated with the passing of each new day. Their friendship had sprouted from a harsh untruth, and then it blossomed into an anaesthetised limbo that they had mistaken for a temporary haven. They shared clothes, make-up, lovers, heart-shaped pills, and Mr Blue the teddy bear. By the time they reached matric they had perfected the intricate art of self-medication. Pot was a kick for kids their age but to them it was the most acceptable implement in a long list of coping mechanisms. People like Sammy drifted in and out of Eve's life almost as frequently as she slipped in and out of reality.

When Eve gained consciousness in Sammy's car the cocaine buzz had worn off, so had the effect of the LSD-laced sangria and the countless champagne supernovas she had knocked back. Sammy's eyes had the opaque quality of the many jaded political animals that had passed through Rosemary's living room in Geneva. That was before she started worshipping at the temple of anti-bacterial cleaning products.

She vaguely remembered sneaking out with Sammy leaving Gavin with his head still in the fridge. When Gavin came out for air to find his girlfriend gone, it did not take him long to jump to the wrong conclusion. There was no trace of them when he went outside to find her. Sammy had ushered Eve into the backseat of a blacked-out Limo and he drove into the night.

"I thought I was having an X-Files trip: the car cruised out of the city and into the countryside chauffeured by a block of a white man with a fat neck." Eve told me in a shaky voice. They had sat in silence past the lights into complete darkness, which was when Sammy decided to speak.

"Today is your lucky day: we are the good guys in this particular game. The next time around you should at least make a fuss before jumping into the `backseat of a car with a complete stranger." Sammy had growled at her unkindly. She just continued staring out into the blackness. "Irish coffee?" he'd asked, pouring hot black coffee out of a silver thermos into matching mugs.

I was as irritated by her recklessness as the stranger that had kidnapped her, "and I suppose you drank the coffee?" I asked.

She nodded and said, "The next thing I know I'm in the passenger seat of Gav's car in your driveway, and he's calling me all sorts of names."

"Are you telling me that you blacked out?" I asked. My eyes were the size of side-plates.

"Gav says Sammy called him and told him to pick me up at the parking lot of some hotel in town-"

"What do you mean by town?' I cut in. I could feel the pressure of the cool walls pressing against my hot skin.

"Down the road town," she replied. It was my turn to barricade my room and freak out in peace for a few days, but that was not an option. I opted for letting all the insanity die-down rather than having my own breakdown in the thick of it. "Keep telling yourself that and you'll end up in the psycho ward of a very remote hospital." Eve commented on my silent, extremely private thoughts.

I was startled by her comment, "What?" I replied

She studied me carefully and said, "You look like my mom when she's resolving not to have a nervous breakdown."

"Look, just finish your weird story so I can figure out a way to get you out of my sight sooner than tomorrow." I said.

She scowled, "Fine. Just so you know; it was Sammy that gave Gavin directions to here, and told him that he'd break his neck in several places if he didn't leave me with you."

"What?"

She smiled, "He'll be back to see us before the end of the week."

I got up and started pacing around the room; it seemed to be getting smaller, "Why?"

"I honestly don't have a clue. All Gav told me is that this Sammy guy instructed him to bring me to you, and said he will come later in the week to talk to both of us. He also said he'd know if we tell anyone else, especially if it's the police."

I hovered above her, "And your boyfriend just obliged like a puppet on a string?" I yelled, with spit flying out of my mouth.

"Well Sammy did threaten his life, that's after he told Gav some intimate details about his family life."

I sat down on the armchair opposite her. "I think you should go home. No offence, but if any of this is true then you're obviously not safe to be around. I can't put four other people in harm's way because of you. "If you're having an episode please check into a good rehab centre because I'm not equipped for any of this shit."

She leaned forward and clasped her arm, her elbows resting on her knees. "Well you better start kitting up because from where I'm standing, this has everything to do with you too. It's not like you picked me up from my gate and brought me here; can't we just freak out about this and get it over with?" she said.

"I need to get some sleep." I retreated to my bedroom.

"Goodnight." She shouted.

I hoped that the sound of my bedroom door slamming shut was a succinct enough response. I tried not to think about Sammy and all the other puzzling omens that came with Eve, but it was proving difficult with all the questions the staff kept asking me. I could no longer assure their safety with all the bombs going off in our midst. "You don't have to be here," I kept telling myself when long forgotten fear got the best of me.

The staff had started whispering and creeping around since the explosion and it got worse after Eve's arrival; which freaked me out even more than it did before. My aunt was ringing me every second minute and Thomas had gone underground; I wanted out, but there seemed to be no exit in sight. Eve was still preparing her own meals in the cottage. Alana's final word was; "she can't have anything from the kitchen unless she fetches it her bloody self!" I had to drive into town to stock up my kitchen after Eve accused me of trying to starve her into being vegetarian. The upside was that Lucia spent all her free time with her, leaving Alana skulking around because Justina and Abe's lips were permanently interlocked. As if that wasn't enough; Justina's loud mouth had spilled everything her big ears had heard, which was a little less than what I knew. I tried telling that to Alana, but she kept threatening to desert me if I insisted on keeping secrets from her. She was even more worried about her ex-husband because it seemed as if his disappearance could be tied to all these strangers that had followed me into her home.

"I've never been up this early on a Saturday morning, not since primary school anyway," said Eve. She was like a big cat on my couch, stretching her long limbs like she had all day to do it.

"What got you up this early; was it raining Ecstasy?" I asked.

"I made a pot of coffee.' She replied, the treacle in her voice suggested that she was back to her old sweet and relatively balanced looking self.

"Your mum rang again." I said.

She sighed and replied, "I know; that's why I've switched my phone off." I tried to talk some sense into her but she raised her hand to shush me. "I've lived with that woman for all my life, and that's twenty years more than anyone else I know. I know her better than I know myself: she can deal with me being here and not speaking to her, but she can't handle the truth."

"Why don't you tell me the truth then; I honestly don't know what the fuck you're talking about?" grumbled. I was incensed. She had literally walked into my living room with all her bogeymen in tow, endangering everyone that was under my supervision.

"I'm sorry, but I didn't ask to be dumped in your living room and confined in this asylum with a bunch of hostile strangers. I'm also a victim here!" she screamed at me.

I sucked in my fury, "fair enough; just bear in mind that the hostile strangers are vulnerable kids that have had enough bizarre experiences in this place. Abe has never touched a water pistol in his life, but he's had a dozen machine guns pointed at him. On top of that the gardener vanished into ether the day after a bomb factory materialised right under our noses-"

She nodded saying, "about people disappearing, I think Sammy might be able to shed all the light you need. He looks like he can make people disappear."

I threw my hands up in defeat. "I must get to work. I'm not quite ready for Sammy to illuminate me on the intricacies of the dark side of life."

 We finished our coffees in contemplative silence and then I left her. I was eager to get away from the weight above my head. The shower invigorated my worn out body and all my mind's anxieties about the insidious stranger that seemed to know it all. "What does he want from us then since he seems to be so in control?" I screamed, loud enough to alarm Eve. She burst in and ripped the shower curtain aside brandishing an empty mug.

"What just happened in here?" she asked?

"I need to meet this Sammy fellow before I lose my mind completely." I replied.

She stared at me as if she was seeing me for the first time, and then she jumped me with a suffocating hug, clinging to my wet body as if her social calendar depended on it. All of a sudden I felt a longing for Thummie's chaotic but ultimately soothing and grounding presence. No amount of pining could shrink the ocean and land mass between me and my best friend, so I adhered to my cousin for solace. We eventually disentangled and I got ready to assume my role as the glue that binds everything. Eve must have been worn down by boredom because she offered to walk me to the manor when I left the cottage.

I regarded her thoughtfully, "only if you stay until after lunch," I said.

"Okay." She chirped eagerly.

I could sense her growing wariness, and did not want her to be left alone with Sammy as the only titbit for her mind to pick at, not if I could help it. "Go find something to wear in my closet; I'll wait for you on the stoep." I said. She came out a picture of femininity in a yellow, strapless summer-dress with a flowing skirt that hung just above the knees. She wore it well; her long legs have the right amount of flesh and curve for her slim frame.

I took her hand in mine and we walked up the path breathing in the orchard.

We found Alana picking coriander for her special curry that has become our traditional Saturday supper treat. Alana read me as if I were a monopoly board; she knew that my boat was in turbulent seas, and did her best to guide me into calmer waters. She squeezed her wee frame between us, her tiny palms on our backs leading us to the kitchen. Lucia cut a lonesome figure; she was deliberately pushing her food around her plate oblivious to the empty chairs around the big table.

"Where's everyone else?" said Eve.

The sound of her voice transformed Lucia into a bolt of lightning; the kind that hugs you and covers you with sloppy kisses. "I'm so glad you came up here." Said Lucia; she only had eyes for Eve.

Just as well because Alana and I had a lot to do before lunch; we were fully booked for the first time. The soft part of me wished Thomas would turn up and take his coffee in the conservatory like the benevolent patriarch we had grown accustomed to. Alana called out my name which was tantamount to her emptying a pitcher of cold water on my face during a peaceful sleep. "It may bend a bit but that porridge isn't going to jump on it by itself," she shrieked like the hag she was. She had made me her first object of ridicule for the day, which served me right for staring at my spoon like a zombie while my mind was on a spontaneous outing. I wanted to lift her of her feet and kiss her, but I was two hundred percent sure she'd bite my lips off. I was grateful to her for the sound of laughter, even though it was directed at me. Everything felt almost normal again;

it was as if Eve had brought nothing else but her healthy appetite and infectious laugh; no demons in her vanity case and no creepy monsters from the family vault.

## Chapter 10

Sammy slipped into the hotel unnoticed during the height of the lunchtime rush posing as a charming customer. I served him a rare steak, and mustard sandwich on rye, and he had angel cake with a cappuccino for dessert. Lucia and Eve assisted Alana in the kitchen, and the smitten couple and I made light work of service. Every table had been wiped down, every bill settled, and all the guests had left, accept for Sammy who was lounging at the bar watching Abe and I go by from behind a cloud of cigar smoke.

"Abe, give me your tray and check on the man that's fumigating the bar. Ask him if he'd like anything else, will you?" I whispered once we were out of earshot.

"I hope he's not staying for supper; Tina and I are going for a swim." He hissed back. The boy shuffled away oozing insolence and irritation; both new traits were by-products of his coupling with "Tina". Alana was unimpressed by the personality transplant and we all knew that. I skipped back to the kitchen with a steaming hot plate of curry on my mind, but my butt was midway to the seat of my chair when the door swung open. Abe's head popped in; "that man wants to speak to you and Eve." He said.

He stuttered when he mentioned Eve's name, turned red, and bailed out the swing doors like a carrot topped lightning bolt. Alana threw a grape at Lucia; it bounced off her pug nose and landed on Eve's sandwich, she picked it up and popped it into her mouth.

Alana winked at Lucia, "I predict trouble in paradise," she said.

"Let's just pretend I'm not here," Justina roared, before storming off to the jungle to lick her wounded pride.

There would have been an awkward silence had Alana not clucked the tune of "love is in the air" with her dentures. My appetite vanished and so did the sandwich's appeal; I pushed my plate aside and motioned for my cousin to eat up and follow me. I was confident that the man in the lounge was Sammy, and I wanted us to get to him before his presence could become a point of discussion. "Lucia it's your turn for afternoon duty; I want you at the bar until six, Justina will relieve you. Eve we better go talk to your friend." I spoke with forced authority to buoy myself for what I presumed would be a rough sail.

Eve got off her chair with my sandwich in her hand, "I can't control my appetite." she explained, trailing two steps behind me. The fact that she was at the rear had nothing to do with the width of the hallway, and everything to do with me being the older sibling. When Sammy saw us coming he got up to his feet beaming like an uncle that remembered to bring sweets. I didn't know whether to shake his hand, or bite it off since he clearly was not expecting the latter. We exchanged names, and then I asked Eve to escort him to the conservatory so I could fix us a pitcher of Long Island Ice Tea.

I found her sitting cross-legged on a cushion on the

the floor with her back to the window seat, and he was in one of the armchairs. I set the tray on the coffee table, placed four cubes of ice in each of the three glasses, and filled them with the potent cocktail. I took my place on the window-seat beside Eve, our backs to the window. We both stared at Sammy; not out of rudeness, but because we genuinely had nothing to say to him. At that point he was just a complicated stranger that seemed to like coffee, alcoholic beverages, fine food and Cuban cigars. He took a long sip from his glass. The room was so quiet we could hear the liquid travelling down to his stomach.

"First I must apologise for alarming you the way I did; I just didn't expect to find Eve around such people." He said, looking genuinely distressed. I nodded to encourage him to speak, but Eve had other ideas.

"So you drugged me and terrorised my boyfriend to get me away from bad company. Is that really your story?" she asked.

"It will all make sense the day you become someone's mother," he replied.

"Well, I'm no one's mother, and you are certainly not my mother!" she laughed hysterically.

"Actually I *am* your father." He said the words with the kind of finality that stops time dead on its tracks.

My scalp started sweating, "are the gods on drugs?" I wondered out loud.

"I can't give you an honest answer on that one, but your cousin is the periodic table of narcotics; she needs to go to rehab." He said.

I could take no more of this man and his self-righteous twaddle. "You must be crazy if you expect me to take you seriously. Do you really expect me to swallow the story of a middle-aged man that's just jumped out of a bush claiming paternity over a fully-grown woman he doesn't know from a bar of generic soap?" I asked him with all the contempt I could muster. It was too much for me to compute that Rosemary was connected to the over-confident man with a solar powered calculator for a heart. I started sobbing from frustration, feeling like a puppet on a string. Eve sat up beside me and stroked my back, "Please go away, you're upsetting her," she sounded each word out like a slow reader.

He refused to leave. In fact, he took control of the situation, and had us both down our drinks insisting that we needed a lot more alcohol in our bodies for what he was about to tell us. I left them to carry on with their hostile banter under the guise of refilling the empty pitcher, dragging my feet to lengthen the time between knowing and blissful ignorance.

"What's wrong" Lucia asked. "You look like you are being chased by a ghost."

"Try ghosts my love." I replied truthfully.

When I got back to the conservatory he had pulled the armchair closer to the window-seat. I flinched at the intimacy, but welcomed the extra privacy it suggested. I couldn't shake off the feeling that Sammy's bombshells needed to be contained within the shrinking space between us. He cleared his throat to speak but all that came out was a sigh accompanied by sadness that sank into the age-lines on his youthful face. Eventually he found his voice, and I discovered that I had been lied to for most of my existence. That Alasdair and all his wretchedness would always be the only uncomplicated thing about my past.

My grandfather Hamish was no ordinary father; I'm not sure if there's anything like him in the animal kingdom. He had four girls with four different women, two of whom had remained devoted wives for their different reasons. It was easier to fall in love with him than it was to get under his skin, a fact that had tragic consequences for two of his young brides. He was a wealthy young science pioneer and a dashing adventurer with glamour and charm on his side. He had romanced Jessica's mother into marrying him two weeks after they started dating. He had the world at his feet and she would be his co-pilot, mate and lifetime apprentice. They had a private wedding ceremony in her parent's garden in Perth, spent the night in his apartment in Edinburgh, and sailed to Japan the next day. Susan Tate's new life seemed like an incredible journey to exotic places and an opportunity for her to explore her senses.

That illusion ended tragically after Jessica's birth was induced in the secluded Peruvian villa that was supposed to be the newlyweds' last stopover before they were to sail home.

On that day Susan had been her usual cheerful self, sitting under a tree cooling her feet in the pond contemplating life with Hamish and the little girl in her stomach. Not once during the pregnancy did they consult a doctor to seek confirmation of the child's development; her husband was her physician. Hamish made the first entry in the baby's diary when Susan was just two weeks pregnant. She had not even missed her period yet, which was why she had laughed the diary off as an endearing manifestation of a man gone broody. When she realised that she was really expecting a child she had questioned Hamish about his certainty about the date of conception. She was adamant to resolve why that entire week had remained a fuzzy flash in her mind. He had put down that glitch in her mind-state to hormonal changes and the amount of time they had spent in the ocean. His rationalisation made sense to her; the world made sense because he was in it.

She was the happiest woman in Peru when she savoured the quiet moment under the shade, and the hint of vanilla in the lemon cheesecake her husband had made as a special treat for her. It never occurred to her that she would wake up the next afternoon with a lifeless belly-bump. She had screamed for Hamish, only to have the Venezuelan maid burst into the room threatening to gaffer tape her mouth shut in perfect English. Susan's world came to an abrupt standstill. It became a nightmare on freeze-frame; she had tried to start the long hike down the mountain to the sleepy town to find a doctor, but ended up on the floor next to the bed. Her legs were useless tubes of jelly that just buckled under the weight of her body. She had been asleep on the floor for over an hour when her husband carried her to the bed. His smell was the same, but the tenderness in his touch had gone.

She had felt his coldness even as he tucked the sheet under her chin, reassuring her that the baby was fine. True to Hamish's predictions Jessica turned out to be a fine looking redhead with big blue eyes. Susan had never stopped wondering who her child had gotten those eyes from. She was too weak to get out of bed and too dry to feed her infant. A month went by and nothing changed, except that Susan died in a horrific car accident. She was cremated in Peru, and Hamish couriered her ashes to Perth for the memorial service before flying the jar to Uig. He spent most of that night in his cabin sitting by the fireside with the telephone on his lap speaking to Bella. She was the woman that had been feeding and loving Jessica from the moment she was taken from Susan's womb.

The following morning Hamish was up before long before his alarm went off and got into his hiking clothes. There was no one around save a solitary fisherman on a rowboat in the middle of the loch when he took a walk. He had the jar of ashes in his raincoat pocket, braving the fog with his deer-hound by his side. He felt a twinge of discomfort as he threw the open jar into the watery expanse; that was the day he went off salmon.

It had already been too late to turn back when it came to his attention that Susan would be a costly mistake. It was six months after Jessica was conceived when he received a telegram from Bella, warning him of the Tate's real profession. Susan's parents were part of an intricate British intelligence counter-terrorism operation. They appeared to be a sensible middle-class couple with a modest accounting firm. In reality, James and Margaret Tate laundered money for Scottish businesses that supported Ulster financially. They were not the timid, middle-aged couple from the countryside his thorough research had revealed them to be. They would be the pesky flies in the ointment he had concocted to bend and stretch Susan's will at his whim. With Susan out of the way permanently Hamish could hold on to his daughter: Keiko and Bella would be waiting on the either side of the world, prepared to share his load.

She had helped him stage Susan's car accident so well they did not need to bribe the police or the coroner. Despite careful planning, things didn't turn out as he had expected. James and Margaret had lost their only child, and could not reconcile with the idea of having him raise their grandchild in another continent. They were determined to fight for joint custody if they had to. Hamish was eating his breakfast when a Cessna carrying the Tate's landed on his private airstrip. They had come to see their granddaughter for the first time.

Margaret was incensed, "Don't you think my grandchild would have been better off with me? What kind of father leaves a baby with strangers in a third world country? What happens when she falls ill?"

Hamish fell straight back into character; he went mad with grief and guilt over his thoughtlessness. It was at that moment that he decided to let the Tates have the child. He told them that he couldn't bear to look at his daughter because the pain of losing his mother was still fresh. James' desire to strangle the life out of him dissipated, but his suspicions remained intact.

Jessica became their new lease on life, another fresh start to soothe their longing for the old country; the Ireland they had left and betrayed to protect the people they love. They were once Noel Christie and Abigail O'Brien, two youths from rural Ireland. It was 1952; Noel was studying for a degree in agriculture in Dublin. He was set to inherit the successful dairy family farm and fulfil his role as the only other Christie male of his generation. Abigail was studying to be a teacher, all she wanted was to settle down and teach primary school.

They met at a dance their respective friends had dragged them to despite their protests. James proposed on their three months anniversary lunch date, and then they went for the walk that changed the course of their lives.
They stumbled upon an IRA rally moments before the army stormed it. They were caught, deemed suspiciously Catholic, and given the choice to either be free captives of the crown or guests in one of her majesty's correctional institutions. They would be tried and convicted as terrorists and their parents'

assets would be seized to "stop their further financial support of the IRA". They did what they thought was best for their families, and stripped themselves of who they had been before they were swallowed by the mob of protestors.

They spent their first six months as property of the crown in a training camp on a small Island in the North Sea. They were then moved to another camp on an island near Anstruther, where they spent another six months before being transferred to their life in Perth. Their accounting practice was right in the city centre, and their Victorian cottage on the outskirts of the town of Dunkeld. At first it was trying to appear as independent business people, knowing that every aspect of their lives was controlled by a handler.

They were expendable cogs of a bureaucratic machine that was wringing the life out of them. It was correspondence learning that helped them maintain some reality in their stage managed life. As futile as amassing a heap of degrees they would never get to use may have seemed, to them the certificates represented an honest relationship with the world outside the lie. Their passion for knowledge and later Susan's activities were the only part of themselves they could share honestly with their friends. Raising her had given true meaning to every second of the day, from when the moment she came into their lives to the day she sailed away. She could have a life outside the invisible walls of the tailor made prison they had been confined in for fifteen years of fabricated misery.

Their twenty-nine years old souls had come out of purgatory the day Uncle Ian brought Susan to their house. She was thirteen and frightened because her parents had just been killed in a car crash. They too had been like the Tates, but luckier because they had produced something of their own that was real. Ian had spun James and Margaret a yarn about failed brakes and a car that flew over a cliff and exploded into little pieces like everything else that was in it. But they knew that Susan's parents had probably become too dangerous to stay alive.

It was two days after the funeral when Ian picked Susan up from a place of safety in central London accompanied by a policeman. She had welcomed the miraculous appearance of an uncle on the worst day of her life. Until that day, all she had known was that both her parents were only children, and that both sets of grandparents were dead. Not in her wildest flights of fancy did she imagine that a living relative would come to whisk her away from solitude and foster care. Ian took Susan's hand in his "I'll take you home now." He'd said, leading her to the awaiting car.

Margaret was sitting in the back unable to take her eyes off Susan as Ian ushered her into the backseat. The child's eyes told a sad tale, Margaret took her into her arms and they stayed that way for most of the journey to Perth.

The young couple was happy to have someone else other than each other; they all needed to be a family for their individual sanity. One evening during Susan's second term of school in Perth, she prepared a treat of brownies and vanilla ice-cream for the Tates and then asked them to adopt her. They in turn twisted Uncle Ian's arm, reminding him that he was part of the reason why life was happening to them instead of them living it. They argued that Susan was as much of a victim of the "car crash" as her parents were. Ian had fast tracked the adoption process because he liked neat packages. That niggling feeling called guilt had nothing to do with his generous spirit. With James' low sperm count and his ageing parents to consider, adopting Susan was a miracle with all the trimmings.

**Chapter 11**

When Hamish had flown away with Susan's ashes Margaret insisted that they had to fight to keep Jessica even if it meant appealing to the man in Ian, their handler. He had called in several favours to clear the Cessna that flew James and Margaret to Uig. Part of him went through all that trouble because to Susan he had been "Uncle Ian" and *that* had nothing to do with the job, but the Tates would never know that. As for whom Hamish McLaughlin really was, that was a matter Ian was instructed not to investigate further. His job was to allay any suspicions James and Margaret may have. All he knew was that Hamish would in fact surrender Susan's baby to Margaret and James. He wasn't surprised when James returned to the plane alone to tell him to fly back without them.

They had flown to Peru with Hamish in the jet he had chartered for fetching Jessica. He had dosed himself with sedatives conveniently slipping into deep sleep until they reached their destination. It was a rested but groggy Hamish that drove them to where Susan had had her accident.

Later that evening Margaret Tate cried until she was hoarse. She was alone in the room her daughter had spent the final month of her life in. For the next two days she collected everything that belonged to Susan, even the odd hairpin that had gotten stuck in the bathroom sink. She couldn't bear to have anything of her daughter's rusting away unnoticed in the remote farmhouse that reeked of long spells of neglect. When her search and salvage mission was complete, she swathed the baby in Susan's canary yellow shawl and they started their journey across the Atlantic.

Jessica flourished under the Tate's care; she started playing the fiddle and piano when she was three. By the time she turned eight she could read music sheets and play every instrument in the Campbell's music room. The Campbell's were an arty family that had bought the adjoining farm when the farmer retired with no heir to leave the land to. At first James didn't approve of them; he had wept like a child when he found out that the neighbour's farm was put on the market.
His own father also had to sell his land to strangers when he grew too old to run Christie's dairy farm. James had locked himself in the study for the entire evening after Ian had delivered the news about the Christies. The handler couldn't make sense of James' fury after he'd delivered what he thought to be good news. Who wouldn't be happy to know that their parents could afford to spend their summers in Ireland, and their winters fishing in the Capo Verde until the end of their days on earth?

That was the day Noel Christie died, so did James' dream of a perfect ending on his dairy-farm with his family. That's the day he accepted that Margaret would always be the only past he could ever have, and that Susan was his future. She was a happy child whose laughter and shrieks of excitement filled the house. It was no surprise to her parents when they found out that she had offered to give the Campbell kids "a tour of nothing" as soon as they stepped out of their dad's Volvo. It was long until an open door policy was established between the two households. So by the time Jess started crawling under the fence to get to the Campbell's music room, it was another set of doting grandparents that received her on the other side of the fence.

John Campbell was a semi-retired professor of music in Sterling University. He started teaching Jessica to play piano when he realised that she was musically gifted. At age six she was already a fully-fledged member of the Campbell Family Band. They held only two concerts per year: The summer concert was always a two days long bank holiday weekend affair that included camping in the barn, and a lot of mud. The winter concert was held in the music room, and everyone slept in the living room. Jessica's love for music flourished in that nurturing environment; her first composition made it to a Ryan's musical. He was a young theatre producer and a first time guest invited by Colette Campbell; she was the youngest child of the family. The next summer Jess played the harp at Colette and Ryan's wedding ceremony. On that day the Campbell gang of teenage grandchildren unanimously concluded that she was destined to have a fabulous life as a "freakishly gifted" individual.

True to their prediction, by the time Jessica turned sixteen she had played in every major traditional and folk music festival in the world. She was awarded an honorary doctorate three weeks after her eighteenth birthday for her research of the accordion in Sotho music. She was on the cover of Rolling Stone and Time's list of a hundred most influential people for four years running.
James and Margaret were the proud youthful grandparents that remained on the fringes of the

spotlight, making the odd family channel and Woman's magazine appearance. Their faces went unnoticed by the people in their past lives; the only trace of their old selves that remained was the colour of their eyes. Not only had they aged, but they had also undergone extensive surgery the year they were extracted from Ireland. They had become new people without roots.

That was until Jessica made good on the promise she had made to herself the day she stumbled on her grandparents' secret in their bedroom. It was on her eighteenth birthday, and she had gone up to her grandparents' bedroom to fetch Margaret's shawl. Had she rushed out she would have missed the tight ball of paper on the marble slab next to the fireplace. Reading that letter that her grandmother had meant to burn was her coming of age experience. It was the saddest record of life in captivity she'd ever read. That became her greatest life affirming discovery, the spark of light that would eventually change her grandparent's life and mine.

She reread the letter several times to let the meaning sink in. She had long accepted that her mother was adopted by the Tates because her biological grandparents had no surviving family. Finding out that her adoptive grandparents were the beleaguered heroes in a Kafkaesque tragedy shifted her perspective and ultimately her purpose. She had spoken to her grandmother the next day, forcing the truth out of her over tea and scones. What she learned made her cut off all contact with Hamish. It was difficult for her to let go of her father, but knowing about the family he had kept hidden from her changed everything. The more she discovered about him was the more she suspected that he was the reason she had no mother. His betrayal was unforgivable in her eyes. She decided to channel her anger into finding the truth.

In the years before she broke up with her father, she had spent many hours imagining her father in different exotic locations around the world. His letters and gifts kept her abreast of where he was until their two weeks of summer adventure; that was when he could do nothing wrong in her eyes.

The Tate's Irish blood ran far back and very thick, Jessica would later find out at the age of twenty-one when she retraced her grandparents' roots under the guise of a tour, and nationwide workshop programme sponsored by UNICEF. It was a hectic six months trek that reached every town and village hall in Ireland. She had stuck to her itinerary to the letter. Uncle Ian's moles had no inkling that she had spent enough time with both sets of great-grandparents to find the snag that could unravel his web.
With Jamie as co-pilot they had planned and survived a kamikaze mission. He was a twenty-six years old attorney with a passion for music and saving the planet. His major ambitions (in his words) were, "to drive nuclear power into the past, and release the stranglehold on the emerging third world economies that keep first world countries lush". His unwavering commitment to a peaceful and just world made him and Jess peas in a pod.

It wasn't just attorney-client privilege that made Jessica trust in him to be discreet about tracking down her-great grandparents. They had been lovers since her eighteenth birthday; that was two days after she employed him as her manager.

When they met he had just dropped out of university after being suspended for organising an anti-Apartheid sit-in that ended badly. This was when the United Nations was pretending to take the moral high ground, which made him just another hippie troublemaker with a lost cause. Lucky for him Jessica was performing in the university's concert hall the night of the sit-in. She heard the news of the arrests and decided to join the small group of parents and loyal friends outside the police station. She had found them milling around holding up placards; tired and helpless as the winter rain beat down on them relentlessly, quietly wearing them down.
She pulled strings to acquire a permit to bask across the road from the police station and kept the vigil going with song and a steady supply of coffee, soup and sandwich rolls. Two days later Jamie and his comrades walked out of the police station more jaded about the existence of justice than they were before they were dragged into their cell. Jessica stayed a day longer to have dinner with the people she had taken in as part of her family during the vigil. That was the night she shook Jamie's damp hand before taking a seat on his right. Initially there seemed to be no fireworks between them, they just enjoyed talking to each other because they had a similar moral outlook on life. She would call him when he had a number, and Jamie would write her long letters that made her linger over every impassioned sentence. He had given up school, and volunteered for a movement that provided crofters

with administrative relief.

"You can still save the world and be my manager you know," she said one night after a packed concert in Aberdeen. She had stated in the five years employment contract that Jamie must finish his law degree within the next two years, or the agreement would be invalid.

"You are truly shitting me. What do I know about managing a living legend?"

She spoke with a thick Jamaican accent; "Unless your letters are packed with lies, then you can manage two legends and several causes at once. I'm tired of being a wunderkind Jamie; make me your cause horse. I have the money and I don't have an appetite for pink slippers with rhinestone studded uppers."

He laughed; teary eyed spouting whiskey out his mouth and nose. "I suppose I should say yes before you drown me in a gulp of whiskey and a spoonful of saliva." He replied and then collapsed in another fit of hysterics.

She took a measured sip of her virgin pina-colada, playing around with the liquid in her mouth before swallowing. The spark that ignited Jamie's heart was born at that precise instant. That would be his divine memory of her, a moment of absolute perfection suspended in time. She noticed and she was happy that he was finally seeing her in that light, relieved that she hadn't been planting her seeds in vain. Later that night he dropped her off at her hotel before driving back to his parents' home in Garelochhead. He arrived at the crack of dawn, physically shattered but too jacked-up to even consider going to bed. He sat in the garden watching the sun rise above the loch and the expanding naval base across the loch. He had watched it mushroom as a little boy, but unlike his peers he didn't remember ever being excited about the industrial activity that came with creating the floating monster. His parents, Michael and Ella Carter, were amongst the locals that felt that the encroaching naval base would change their way of life forever. They still remembered seeing the live visuals of what happened in Hiroshima and Nagasaki when they were younger. They would always associate that horror with nuclear power.

Michael Carter's great-grandfather, Joseph, settled in Garelochhead in the late 1850's at the beginning of the steamer era. He was an eighteen years old boy charged with building and running the family hotel, another venture his father had decided to invest a small part of his sizeable fortune into. Their wealth could be traced back to the North American colonial wars; the Carters had jumped at every opportunity to turn conflict into wealth. They had been turning blood into doubloons since King William's War. The men were tough as diamonds, quick minded, and they had money magnets coursing through their veins. Joseph had always been different from the rest of his brothers. He had the Carter balls and business aptitude but had a more bohemian outlook on life by family standards. Sending him to Scotland was his father's way of cutting him some slack. He had given Joseph the freedom to either sink or swim in his own inimitable fashion. Once free of expectation Joseph flourished like a fungus on a damp facecloth in a dark cabinet.

He built a small theatre as part of his hotel: it's that vision that kept his life's work alive over a century later when some local hoteliers had resorted to burning down their own establishments from sheer desperation. By manifesting his dreams he handed down an intact way of life to generations. He died in his sleep in 1932 aged ninety-two. The Carter eventually evolved into an ethical entrepreneurship hub with Jessica as its epicentre after her husband had taken over the reins from his ageing parents.

But that morning in the garden Jamie still had no clue how tightly he and Jessica's destiny was sewn up. He was still fact-checking in case the whole thing was a hallucination, a result of the vast quantities of LSD he had taken two years earlier.

"I guess it's a good morning judging by the grin on your face," his father's voice was accompanied by the smell of just-brewed Carter roast. Morning coffee in the garden was another family tradition that dated back to the first day Joseph saw the sunrise from where his home would stand. Jamie and Michael sipped in silence taking in the electricity in the air. There was no doubt that something huge had dropped out of the sky and onto his son's lap, and Michael could no longer contain his curiosity as to exactly what it was. "Come on, out with it!" he had said.

**"My life is finally living up to my imagination dad; I'm that cheesy bloke that's living the dream."**

**Chapter 12**

## Daddy's Girls

Unlike Jessica, Kwezi was daddy's girl. She was unflinching in her commitment to being the means to Hamish's ends. Her mother was Angel; she was a third year botany student when she left her studies to marry Hamish. She met Hamish at a Communist Movement meeting that was held in her sociology professor's living room. Hamish' presence had made angel so uncomfortable, she censored her progress report on the party's activities in Soweto. There was something about him that didn't seem quite right to Angel's probing eye.

That night she felt vulnerable in the cottage that had been her home since her first year in a catholic school for girls. She was thirteen when she moved into the cottage that belonged to her father's employer, Graham Gibson. He was also her tuition fees sponsor, and had taken it upon himself to give all of Angel's siblings the same opportunities his children had. The Msibi home in Soweto was crammed full of books and board games, and the children spent every weekend with the Gibsons experiencing the privileges of the other side of the racial divide.
The nature of Graham Gibson's service to both the South African and American governments gave the Msibi children a free pass to racially demarcated zones their black peers had no access to. They had gone whale watching in Hermanus, walked on the Great Wall of China and explored Giza in a caravan of dromedaries guided by Bedouins. Their world was bigger than the pinhead sized peep-hole they

were meant to look out of into the rest of the world from the shrinking space they had inherited from colonialism.

Angel could still feel the heat of Hamish's eyes boring into the back of her head when she slipped into her bed after the meeting. She tossed and turned unable to find stillness, not for fear that her communist activities could turn her siblings' world upside down. It was Hamish' sudden presence that was responsible for her nightmares. She had always been careful in concealing her extracurricular activities from the Gibsons. After all Graham's name was a permanent feature on the lists of government operatives that made their way to the hands of her comrades; he was one to be wary of.
She had found it surprisingly easy to be herself around him, something she ascribed to the fact that he had never been her favourite Gibson. Not because he was less kind than the others, in fact he was the most sensitive member of his family. She simply couldn't find the "on" switch for trust when it came to him. It was Graham that noticed the darkness around her eyes the next morning at the breakfast table.

"What's wrong Angel," he'd asked.

"Final year pressure is finally catching up with me; don't worry I'll outrun it." She replied, motioning with her hands.
They laughed and the attention turned back to Allison's looming matric exams. She was the youngest and the most likely to turn into an outright saboteur. Allison was an outwardly sulky but sweet

teenager with strong opinions about the immoral regime her father was serving. In her private conversations with Angel, she referred to her father as "the pseudo-liberal fascist next door". Angel winked at her and excused herself from the breakfast table.

She sucked in a lungful of the Jacaranda scented morning air as she drove out in her jalopy. By the time she reached the bottom of the road she was already singing along to the radio. She almost didn't stop at the traffic lights when she realised that the driver of the car on the other lane was Hamish. He was motioning for her to stop, so she pulled over to find out what he was after. Three months later she was in Zimbabwe, knocked up and married to a man she hardly knew. She was not in love with Hamish; she was with him because that was where she had to be. She was six months pregnant when he left her in their new home in Port St Johns, only to return when Kwezi was three months old. That would be the first of a series of disappearances in their time together.

 Angel had known better than to care about anything else other than her child and making a living independent of Hamish. The money he left her during his disappearances went into fertilizer, seeds and eventually farming equipment when Angel had saved up enough. She became a vital link of a chain of village women that would not bend to their difficult circumstances. She flourished   as Hamish went about the business of weaving his web. He was the father of her child, so she never discussed him with the other women. She was careful not to allow the village into the queen-size bed she shared with her daughter, or the fact that she only communicated with Hamish out of necessity. She spent the rest of her time at home, either playing with Kwezi or catching up with the administrative duties of the farming co-op she had initiated. It had become a necessity since the men of the village were either lost in the big cities or working in the mines. Some were only seen over the Christmas holidays, others not at all. A lot of the women stopped receiving money and packages when their men opted for starting new, self-contained families in the city; Angel was merely one of many grass-widows. The exodus of muscle and protection left some of the younger wives with no option but to leave the village in search of their men. They left their children under the supervision of older relatives and neighbours, and worked as maids in the cities to fill the gap left by their menfolk. Those that stayed weathered the hardship until the co-op provided a reprieve from growling stomachs and testy children.

Despite Hamish's money Angel felt as impoverished as the abandoned women. That feeling gnawed at her spirit until she decided to use some of what she had given up to take back what was left of her life and it her own again. The rest of it belonged to Hamish, and yet she still couldn't make sense of why she had let it happen without a fight. Loving Kwezi made it impossible for her to dwell on their unlikely union, and easier for her to accept that she had indeed turned her back on everything she was to rear a child for Hamish. After Kwezi's seventh birthday the series of events that occurred since the day she had pulled over to the side of the road to chat with Hamish started haunting her.

Hamish had doted on Kwezi from the first instant he gazed into her blue eyes. She was a beautiful baby with skin like milky coffee and an upturned canopy of long black lashes for her blue eyes. She had the power to make his cold eyes smile with genuine warmth and pleasure. Angel took comfort in the healthy relationship between father and child, even after Kwezi's third birthday. That was when Hamish took to going away with her for weeks. She would return with new words and tastes that had the whole village fascinated and often disgusted. Angel was almost happy, and then one day she woke up to an empty bed, Hamish had left with her greatest source of light.

She was cast adrift with only the village women to hang on to. At first she had allowed them to convince her that he'd be back, that he always came back. She waited patiently from one harvest to the next, until her patience waned and all the seasons became one long winter. She lost more weight as the skeletons tumbled out of the closet that Kwezi's presence had kept firmly shut. She was left alone to pick at each sack of bones intently, piercing together the clues that lead to her picturesque grave in the wild coast. It pained her to wake-up every morning knowing the truth yet remaining powerless to change anything. She could only pray that Hamish would return her child, that only then would he be swallowed by the sea. She cried herself to sleep every night trying to think herself out of her cage.

Graham Gibson had made sure that all ties with her family were permanently severed. That was soon after she discovered that she was pregnant, and decided that she would keep the child and raise it by herself. She'd had no intention of marrying Hamish. Sleeping with him could only have been an unfortunate lapse of judgement on her part; she didn't remember how it had happened. Angel was frantic when she discovered that she was pregnant; she faced certain prosecution for having a white man's child and it would be removed from her care. She was relieved when Graham agreed to meet her in private to discuss her "predicament". The last thing she expected was for him to suggest that she do whatever Hamish wanted of her.

"Your extramural activities could get a lot of people in some serious shit. I suggest you put the potential consequences before what you want or don't want." He had told Angel over cappuccino and chocolate cake at the Rand Hotel. She was devastated, unable to make head or tails of the situation she found herself in.

"But Graham, you must help me." She had pleaded with him. She was helpless; the tears streaming down her face were her last resort.

His eyes were drained of all their familiar kindness; Graham was at work. "You gave up that privilege when you started your second life as an errand girl for the communists." He spat the words out slowly, filling the air between them with mutual contempt and disgust.

He had engineered Hamish into Angel's life and she couldn't get rid of either of them. Angel had always known that Graham was grooming her and her siblings into the elite black citizens that his employers needed to help maintain the status quo. What she did not realise was that Graham had been over the moon when he was made aware of her involvement with the communist party. He had kept an eye on her by twisting the sociology professor's loyalties; he made him choose between betraying his ideals and his family's wellbeing. Graham had painted a graphic picture of the harassment the professor's family would have to endure. A treason charge and a future of random house arrest orders for his family was more than the professor could bear. Some of his comrades were already sentenced to life in solitary confinement in what he could only describe as a maximum security penile colony for men. He no longer had the option of taking his children on an indefinite "anthropological excursion" to the Soviet Union. He was under the military intelligence radar, every breath he took was carefully monitored and analysed for traces of communism. He had no power to challenge Graham when he pushed Hamish into his inner sanctum.

"Don't worry professor; we run a flawless outfit. Your foreign guest's background is as solid as the Berlin Wall." Graham had assured the miserable man. He didn't take pleasure in reducing the scholar to a quivering mess, fear was merely an occupational tool that yielded the best results at the worst of times. "That's all for now, thanks professor," he had said, before letting himself out of the office leaving his victim with the titan task of pulling himself together. He never did, he gassed himself in his garage a few years later.

*The conservatory was almost in complete darkness by the time Sammy was done talking. We could barely make out each other's shapes in the dwindling light. Eve and I had not said a word in three hours; the only thing that passed through our lips were the liquids we ingested and the smoke we blew out.*

"When was Kwezi returned to her mother?" I asked Sammy, more frightened than I had ever been before. I realised that all I remembered was the moment of the explosion, everything else I thought I knew was filled in by Jessica over the years.

He took both my hands in his and said, "That is something you should discuss with Marcia. She's a great psychologist; gets good results and is highly recommended."

It took me a week to warm up to the idea of paying someone to play with my mind. I did not trust the hypnotherapist, but realised that I had to give in for her to help unlock the memories of my childhood. Marcia was a medium built, uptight girl with masses of neatly twisted locks that framed her face. She looked like a pitch black mop with a brown generously-padded face that scrunched up into a mask of discomfort when she was being assertive. She stayed at the hotel for three weeks as a "guest" that spent an inordinate amount of time with me in my cottage. Sammy insisted on paying for her accommodation, her meals and my hypnotherapy sessions.

I was in a permanent frazzled state trying to keep my

X-Files sessions from Alana. She smelled a rotten fish and she would not rest until she had disposed of it.

"Why does this Marcia spend so much time alone with you; are you two lesbian or what?" she sneered when she had finally cornered me in the tiny bar.

I looked at her with feigned confusion, blowing her off with a long list of kitchen duties so I could slip away to the green house to meditate under the false pretence of tending to Koos' plants. His nursery had become my sanctuary at a time when reality seemed more twisted than fiction. I was more confused than I had ever been; I was no longer sure which of my experiences were real. I was still coming to terms with the fact that the mother I saw splattered on the walls of the house that was in all my nightmares was Angel and not Kwezi. The biggest frustration for me was not having any recollection of the blue-eyed woman that had given birth to me, or how I ended up with Angel if the last time she had seen my mother was twenty-three years before I was born?

The snippets of laughter in the sunshine and whiffs of cocoa scented winters that were dredged up by my subconscious did nothing to fill the gaps with missing truths. I was certain that Jessica and Jamie had all the answers in a discoloured envelope, just waiting for me to be ready for its contents. I made the choice to not have my parents catch the next flight to Johannesburg so they could mollycoddle me to extinction. Thomas, my biological father who had sprouted out of the African landscape was the most logical source of information for me to tap into.

It had taken another two weeks of therapy and a blood test for me to come to terms with the fact that the indispensible taxi driver is my father. Acceptance didn't abate the anger I felt towards him.

I sat alone in Koos' dwarf jungle of mango, avocado, pawpaw and pineapple trees, inspired to tame my world by lighting up every dark corner. I could not stumble around with a blindfold on and take care of Eve at the same time. She needed to find the right answers as much as I did, but I had to make the six years between us count for something.

"They said I'd find you here," said Thomas' voice from behind me.

Where did you learn your creeping technique?" I asked when I was done shrieking out of my skin. We had gone past his shame, my anger and my confusion. It became more important to us to love each other when we finally acknowledged that Kwezi had turned both our lives upside down. Falling into his embrace had become as natural as taking one step after the other. "I really need to talk you." I told him as I disentangled myself from his horrendous sweater.

"Rosemary," he explained, pointing at the squint-eyed purple kitten that was curled-up on his belly. "What did you want to talk to me about?" he asked.

The look on my face gave it all away. He sighed and motioned for me to sit on the wooden bench at the centre of the fragrant forest. It felt delightfully awkward to sit taller than my father and the trees with their plump fruit. The setting was loopy enough to make anything that came out of Thomas' mouth conceivable. Anything to do with Kwezi and Hamish seemed to blur the line between reality and science-fiction.

I was not surprised to learn that my life with Angel started with her finding me tucked in an insulated banana box on her doorstep. Angel had instantly recognised the big blue eyes that stared back at her when she picked up the wailing bundle in the fruit box. She knew then that Kwezi was alive and feared that someday the baby she was holding would also be stolen away from her. It was her resolve to keep me safe that drove her back into the liberation movement.

The son of one of her co-op partners was a Fort Hare graduate but couldn't find work, so he had joined the co-op. He also arranged safe-houses for revolutionaries that were either slipping in or out of the country. He had tried to enlist Angel's help once, but she had made it clear that she was sympathetic to the cause but wanted nothing to do with it. That was before she had a reason to fight to keep her granddaughter safe from Hamish's clutches. He would return someday and Angel wanted to be prepared for that day; she would not be caught off-guard and be imprisoned by fear again. Soon after she had made that decision her house became one of the underground lighthouses whose reputation finally reached Jessica and Jamie's dinner table. One evening chance brought them an overnight guest from South Africa called Sizwe. He was about the same age as they were, extremely intelligent and highly strung-out. Jessica's stomach had tightened when he told her about how and why he had kidnapped and then abandoned his blue-eyed two years earlier. She had a feeling that the child Sizwe was talking about could be a link to Hamish. That night she had promised Sizwe that she would do everything in her power to rescue the child, and assured him that Hamish would think twice before taking anything away from her.

Jessica believed that her father was incapable of loving anyone more than he loved his work. She had made that conclusion three years earlier when Uncle Ian summoned her to his bedside. He was dying of pancreatic cancer, and was itching to lighten the load on his conscience. He confessed that Hamish had been his obsession since Susan's death. He knew why Hamish had murdered her, all he needed was for him to confess how he had done it . Jessica contacted Hamish and confronted him with every scrap of information uncle Ian had handed over to her; he responded by falling off the face of the earth. That prompted her to invest a sizeable amount of her fortune in following every lead that may have brought her closer to finding Hamish, sending her deeper into Uncle Ian's world. The more she unravelled was the more intricate her father's web of deceit seemed to become.

The night she found out about my existence she dropped everything to go and find Angel. She immediately started planning a trip to South-Africa, using her contacts for an inconspicuous entry into the police state. Of course Angel didn't trust Jessica at first; she wouldn't even take comfort in the familiar eyes and their peculiar shade of blue. She was also deaf to the reassurances of the comrade that had accompanied the young woman to her doorstep; Angel knew very well that anyone that everyone is capable of betrayal. She may have given the comrade's best friend shelter until safe passage had been arranged for him, but she expected no loyalty in return. She clammed up using cool politeness as a shield against her visitors.

Jessica would not leave; she stayed in a rental cottage on second beach long after her escort had been smuggled back to Bloemfontein. She visited Angel every single day, but there was still no trace of the blue-eyed child. A search and destroy team could have ripped the village apart, and they would have come out with nothing. Angel was intent on keeping her grandchild safe from Hamish's clutches. She cooked lunch for Jessica for everyday of the duration of her stay. Her eyes had filled with compassion when Jessica told her mother's story, but she still wouldn't budge in her resolve to "keep the child out of it." Eventually they had their last meal together, and on that day Angel gave Jessica a picture of the blue eyed child.

"Maybe one day she will end up at your doorstep, but right now I feel it is better that you two don't meet," she said.

Jessica respected her wishes; they kept contact through letters that journeyed from hand-to-hand across the ocean. A few years later Jessica received a telegram alerting her that the cottage was available for the summer, she knew that it was her cue to pay someone to make the child disappear within forty eight hours. Angel's pieces were found with the charred remains of a little girl who had drowned in a well a few days earlier. Sightings of a strange boat and the accidental drowning of a local child sparked a plan that Angel could only pull off with Jessica's complete cooperation.

**Chapter 13**

Thomas took my trembling hand in his and steadied it with a brave smile. "I'm hungry," he said, rubbing the scrawny elongated cat as he led the way to the kitchen.

We found Abe and Lucia mashing peas for the day's traditional fish and chips special. There was a civil servant workshop in town. So we had a café full of clean shaven black men in ill-fitting, tailored Italian suits wolfing down generous portions of hake.

"We only have ten pieces left; if they order any more offer them cottage pie and Greek salad," Alana snapped at Justina as she popped out to take more orders.
The tiny titan was stationed in front of the portable fryer with a glass of cold water, a sheet of grease proof paper, a neat stack of fish and a bowl of batter placed within her limited reach. I washed my hands and started cutting up portions of the fresh shepherd's pie that was in the terracotta baking tray Alana had left on the prep table.

Eve waltzed in and dumped another load of dishes in the cluttered sink and placed orders for shepherd's pie and salad. I prepared the plates of food and an extra one for Thomas who had retreated to Eve's favourite spot on the doorstep. He ate slowly staring into the vegetable garden as if the neat rows of plants held the answers to all the questions in his troubled mind.

Later that evening Eve and I sat on the deck with a 1.5 litre jug of punch to celebrate the end of my sessions with Marcia. I must say I missed her presence as much as I was relieved that I had my mind to myself again.

"She must be the loneliest woman in hell," I thought out loud.

Eve took a long sip of her drink, "we won't know that until we know for sure," she said, raising her glass in a silent toast. She captured my heart whole. I would bargain with my life to make sure that she is never touched by evil again. "Why are you looking at me like that?" she asked, laughing.

"I love you little sister." I said.

She raised her glass, "Ditto," she grinned baring her milky pearls for all the stars to see.

I could no longer keep the truth about our grandmother to myself. I decided to let Eve in so she could decide how far she was willing to get to the bottom of why our lives were so complicated. She was still smiling but her eyes had stopped laughing. "What's wrong?" she asked.

"I don't know where to start," I replied.

"Why don't you start with your sessions with the head mechanic?" she suggested.

At first I struggled to find the right way to share my childhood memories with her, but the words flowed and my voice had steadied by the time I got to relay my last conversation with Thomas. Her eyes inched out of their sockets a bit more as the story of our lives unfolded.

"I still don't know how Sammy and my mother fit into all of this?" she said, breaking the long contemplative silence.

"That's why I don't think we can put off seeing her for much longer. This cloak and dagger stuff is driving me up the wall." I replied from some place far away from the stillness of Parys.

"I need to sleep on that," she said and then she left without saying goodnight.

I would not allow her to shut Rosemary out any longer, but I let her sleep secure in the illusion that she would talk to her on her own terms in her own time. I spoke to rosemary that night, and she agreed to meet me in a small Greek restaurant I suspected she had selected for its spotless white decor. The next morning I set off to our rendezvous; she was already a bit tipsy when I arrived so I decided to meet her half way. I had booked into a nearby bed and breakfast for the night with the soul intention of drinking my aunt out of her shell. Eve had warned me that a good bottle of chardonnay was one way of thawing the ice queen. The small talk was excruciating, and Rosemary was the first to admit to that.

"I'm not very good at breaking ice, or anything else for that matter." She giggled into her half-full glass of chardonnay.

"I need to order some food, and a strong drink," I confessed to a dark skinned waiter in a very white t-shirt and matching jeans.

I ordered a double whisky and soda and tapas for two. She waited for me to wolf down most of the platter's contents, before unburdening herself of the truth she'd been trying to clean off with industrial detergents for twenty miserable years.
Rosemary had been impulsive and naive in her youth. She had let Kwezi into her life, who thanked her by turning her world upside down. She was a twenty-one years old idealist with her head in the clouds of Azania when she met Kwezi by "accident" at Allison Gibson's wedding reception. She didn't recall how they got to speak about their families, but she has vivid memories of their conversation beside the Gibson's swimming pool. They had slipped away from the revellers in the garden, leaving behind the fairy lights and the jazz band for a sober moment that would change Rosemary's life irrevocably. Kwezi had lied eloquently about everything, including Angel's disappearance. She painted a tale of a sad girl that had left everything for love only to realise that she had gained the world but had lost the right to share it with her family. She twisted Hamish's betrayal into a love story that featured Apartheid as the chief villain, and Angel as another victim of the long arm of the Special Branch. Rosemary wept for the aunt she never met, and then celebrated finding her sister. They chatted until the sun came out, and still there was so much more they needed to say to each other. Kwezi had begged her

not to compromise her by letting the rest of the family know about her existence.

"I don't want to suffer the same fate as my mother, or worse." She had added to ascertain the gravity of her plea for discretion.

"You can trust me with anything." Rosemary assured her.

That moment was the beginning of her descent into the abyss; she was completely under her cousin's spell. Kwezi's light complexion, fine curls and blue eyes allowed her to pass herself off as an Israeli. She'd bought a house in a quiet Johannesburg suburb, and soon after the pool party Rosemary was spending all her free time there posing as her translator. They had become closer and inseparable; accept for when Kwezi would disappear for days or weeks on end.

She had allowed Rosemary to assume that her absences were the result of her clandestine work with the liberation movements. Rosemary's boyfriend was in the movement; he did a lot of disappearing and she'd learned not to ask questions. She was unaware that Kwezi was using the Gibson's political connections to further a greater agenda like her father before her.

It was important to him that his bloodline be carried through Kwezi; his other daughters were infertile. "I wasn't given sons, I was blessed with daughters." He would often say when he gave talks on artificial insemination and genetic engineering.

Kwezi was desperate to give her father the

granddaughter he needed to affirm that he was worthy of his lifetime. Although she was fertile, she could no longer carry a child to full term. Rosemary was the key to her redemption, she would help repair the damage caused by the butcher that had delivered Kwezi's first child.

One morning after a rowdy party at an actor's house Kwezi broached a bizarre subject as he ate pancakes and bacon.

"Would you carry a child for me?" she asked Rosemary.

Rosemary chewed thoughtfully. "Hypothetically I would, but I don't see how it's possible."

At first when Kwezi explained the procedure, Rosemary thought she was pulling her leg. Kwezi bolted out of the room and returned with diagrams and photographs. That was when Rosemary realised that her cousin was serious. "I can't carry a child, and that's the one thing that's missing in my life." Kwezi had said, and then she crumbled before her cousin's eyes. That was enough to convince Rosemary that by helping Kwezi she would be fulfilling a greater purpose.

The procedure seemed simple enough; hiding the pregnancy from her parents would be their biggest challenge. A fabricated gap year sponsored by the Gibson's gave them sufficient cover, but Graham's part in the charade didn't raise any suspicions in Rosemary's mind. She was too busy preparing her body for its precious cargo to question her benefactor's reasons for entangling himself in the elaborate scam that could go badly on so many different levels. It was only when drunk on watered down wine twenty-one years later that she realised how her devotion to her cousin had reduced her to a self-destructive idiot.

There were laws against cross-racial love, but the apartheid government had not considered the advent of a black woman carrying a white woman's egg that was fertilised by a black man's stolen seed. The punishment for that unchristian crime would have been severe.

Sammy could not have imagined that Rosemary was harvesting his sperm for Kwezi when he used a condom like he had always done for the two years they'd been lovers. Kwezi's only specification was that the donor must be healthy, and Sammy was the poster boy for wellness. He believed that the earth revolved around Rosemary and would have given her anything she desired. He would have gladly ejaculated into a dozen plastic cups if that would have made her happy. He was unaware of her intentions, and surprised when she asked for a break from their relationship.

"How long is a break?" he'd asked. She made a lame excuse about needing a year to sort herself out. He was confused, and had suspicions that the sudden change in her attitude had something to do with the new friend she was keeping under wraps. He only got his explanation when she turned up on his doorstep eight months later.

Kwezi had moved with Rosemary to a farm in

Broedestroom; the small holding was unknown to her South-African associates and her foes. They had gone through a lot of trouble to stage their departure to Israel. Rosemary was to spend part of her "gap year" in a kibbutz, and the rest of it exploring the middle-east with her wealthy sponsor. No one else other than Kwezi and Graham knew where she'd really gone to. As her belly grew bigger she started wondering what kind of a mother Kwezi would make, and why she had access to cutting-edge fertility research. At first Kwezi dismissed her questions as the result of a "hormonal head rush", and then her disappearing spells grew longer and closer between. Rosemary's hormonal head rush persisted; she did not know what to make of one plus one, but she realised that she had to keep her freedom to take long drives in the countryside unaccompanied by Kwezi or one of her drivers. She threw herself into her studies, and stopped asking any questions her cousin wouldn't provide answers for. It didn't take her long to slip back into the rhythm of her life before Kwezi came in playing a different tune. She had always studied from home since she couldn't find a place in any of the prestigious universities. One cloudy afternoon she had left the house intending to take her usual short drive, but maternal instinct propelled her even further; she drove to Rustenburg with no intention of ever returning.

Sammy had taken her in hoping that she would say that the child she was carrying was theirs; after all she had been out of his radar for just under eight months. He had the mind to throw her out when she confided the peculiar ruse to him, but he did not have the will to discard his unborn child. He could not change the fact that Kwezi had used him to make a child, but he had the power to shape the child's future.

He had arranged for Rosemary and her belly to vanish into the heart of Soweto via the backwoods of Norway. He had helped her change her last name and her face, grateful that his child had inherited his dark skin and brown eyes. Where could a black woman have gone unnoticed raising a fair skinned child with blue eyes? Sammy provided for Eve but kept away from her; it was the only way he could keep her safe from Kwezi's obsession.

"What happened to you and Sammy?" I asked.

Rosemary drained her glass before responding. "He fell out of love with me and made room for forgiveness; I'm still trying to live with what I did." She replied.

The boulder that stood between us crumbled from the intensity of the conversation we'd had. We were the last customers to leave the restaurant. She had agreed to room with me for the night, so we could continue our long overdue conversations. She told me about the family, and asked me about my life in Scotland. I told her about my divorce, and that was the first time I laughed about it without feeling a twinge of pain. The hardest thing for me was telling Eve the truth about our mother. There are no right words to tell a person that everything she knows about herself is false; she was in too stunned to shed any tears. I let her mope around my cottage for a few days, gave her the space to let the truth sink in at her leisure. And then one evening she decided to put her anger away and she called Rosemary for the first time in two months.

"That woman gave her life to me, literally." I was taken aback and confused by Eve's words, and she must have read that on my face. She said, "I love you, and we need to find our mother so our parents can be free of us."

I nodded in agreement, "bloody secrets have a way of losing their potential to cause harm when they are out in the open, but we have to be clever and extremely careful. Our mother has the maternal instincts of a wolf spider."

The next morning Sammy called and asked me to clear the hotel for the whole day.

"Why do *we* have to go to Johannesburg for the afternoon? What are you two up to?" Alana's eyes were suspicious slits of fury.

I leaned forward to meet her slits with my bulging eyes. "Just take the bleeding day off and stop questioning my motives. The car has a full tank of gas and I'll give you pocket money. If you won't go to Joburg, then find something else to do anywhere else but here."
Justina grinned from ear to ear relishing the responsibility of being the captain of their journey to the city. That was only because she had a drivers' licence and she knew her way around the city. Lucia and Abe were just as excited if not more, but they were too sensitive to Alana's feelings to let their eagerness show. I felt like an ogre forcing an outing

to a bustling city on an old lady that had just found the nerve to venture to neighbouring farms after years of never leaving her own backyard.

"I'm sorry Alana, but you can either take this as a healthy step forward or hide in the backseat under a blanket until it's over." My voice was gentler and my eyes were melting in their sockets, but hers grew considerably colder. "I really need you to do this for me Alana, it's too much to ask but I know you'll handle it as well as you do everything else." I smiled weakly, and she pelted me with a piece of her toast.

"Can we eat now?" Eve pointed at her untouched pile on a plate, barely visible under the load of protein and starch.

"Your alien tapeworm colony is expanding," Alana cackled our world back onto its wonky axis.

I locked the gates as soon as they had driven off; relief passed over my body lifting my feet off the ground. In less than two hours I'd be sharing a meal with my parents, my father, my aunt and my half-sister's father; it would the first large gathering of my maternal family.

"This feels unreal; how many people go through such pains to keep a family meeting a secret?" Eve rambled on, banging pans and spoons to punctuate her sentences. I could have strangled her for squeezing the joy out of the day. "Doesn't it freak you out that they've managed to keep each other's existence a secret from us for all this time; it's like finding out that you were stolen from your cot while your parents were watching McGyver in the living room."

 The fragile chain that held my patience together finally snapped. "No Eve, it's not the same thing. Rosemary *is* your mother; she carried you for nine months and brought you into this world. She raised you into this beautiful, intelligent, self-absorbed young woman you are. Would you rather she had given you back to a woman that only wanted you as a peace offering to her father? I ended up on Angel's doorstep because she's too selfish to care for anyone else other than herself. Just be grateful for Sammy and Rosemary's guts, his connections and everything they've done to keep your big head safe from the rest of your insane family." I stormed off to fix myself a hard drink.

Jessica looked older than she had six months earlier. "You must be tired from the flight, shouldn't you sleep first?" I said, fussing over her.

She squeezed my hand reassuringly, "I've been in Johannesburg for two weeks now my pet," she said.

Silence swept over the table again, the first time around Eve had wondered out loud about people's sanity. Eve and I exchanged weary looks and waited for someone to volunteer an explanation.

"We are very sorry Ceillidh, but we had to take every precaution; strange things started happening after you left home." Jamie explained.

We fixed our eyes on him, eager to be filled in with

details. I trusted Jamie because he couldn't tell a lie with a straight face, which was a noble trait when the truth is lean. He explained that Jessica had started feeling like she was being watched by more than the usual cast of spooks haunting the Faslane area. They had contacted nan Tate, who confirmed that their phones were tapped, and that all the computers that were connected to the internet were transmitting to a remote computer. My grandmother made minced meat of triangulating the exact location of the hacker; her discovery sent shockwaves across the Atlantic.

The three ring circus of intrigue rolled back into action when all the players received the dreaded call; that was on the day Thomas "found" my relatives. Hamish was the reason behind Thomas' frequent visits to my aunt's house, the intimate conversations that puzzled Eve, and Rosemary's skittishness. What Eve had suspected to be a lovers' reunion was actually a mobilisation drive. It became clear to me why Rosemary had insisted that her daughter would be better off with me on the farm. While Rosemary was doing her best to hold on to her wits, Jessica and Jamie were planning a trip to China with the sole purpose of losing Hamish's bloodhound in the heart of Beijing. When they were rid of their human tail, Sammy's influence opened a discreet doorway into South-Africa.

"I prayed that this would never happen, especially after all you have been through. Apart of me believed that he had done us all a favour and died" Jessica's voice was as shaky as her hand.

I took it in my steady one, happy to be her pillar for a change. "You did your best: I'm glad I know. I can finally get rid of that niggling feeling that something bad is lurking in the shadows." I said.

Jamie winked at me, smiling like the proud dad he had always been. Eve sat between her parents drumming an impatient rhythm on the table with her long fingers. "So, what now?" she asked.

All eyes instinctively turned to Sammy. He and Kwezi had been moving in the same circles since the first democratic elections. They had recognised each other instantly, but he had been the first to ask about Rosemary's whereabouts. As far as Kwezi was concerned he had no idea that his girlfriend had been pregnant at the time of her disappearance. She had jumped at the opportunity of giving Sammy's company a five years security contract, like every other home owner in her suburb had done. To Kwezi Sammy represented much more than protection for her jewels and silverware; he would eventually unearth the elusive trail to Rosemary's doorstep. She was certain that her cousin would resurface just like everyone else in her old crowd had.
The frightened, impassioned, brave and naive young men and women she had met during the liberation struggle had evolved into self-assured captains of industry and omnipotent politicians. The cobbled upmarket streets and rambling mansions finally belonged to them, and they feared nothing. It's the new mood of fearlessness that assured Kwezi her cousin would turn up; she was certain that she and the child had been kept safe by money and political influence. She put Sammy's name on top of the

outgoing list of invitations for membership in her private club. That's how she had wrapped her strings around everyone else that had a number 55 Hunter Street access card.

Unlike the other patrons of Kwezi's club, Sammy did not take drugs, conduct dodgy deals or indulge in "discreet" orgies. He knew about the hidden cameras because he had never taken his eyes off Kwezi. As liberation movement's Chief of Domestic Security and Intelligence Operations he's always had the man power and means to maintain surveillance on his subject. Jessica's contacts also provided regular reports that kept his side ahead of the game. Despite all their effort, Hamish's whereabouts remained a mystery. His face smiled back from his wedding picture which was taken in the Tates' garden in Perth less than a year before Jessica was born. The other picture was taken at a pharmaceutical conference in Geneva twenty years earlier; that's the last time he was seen in public. He didn't even attend his Japanese daughter's funeral.

Momo had died when her light-aircraft was swallowed up by the earth during take-off. The private airport's owners were only too pleased to oblige the family's request for them to handle the accident discreetly. The accident wasn't even reported to the aviation authorities; it just didn't take place.
Isabella was the most visible of Hamish's children, she ran the biggest cosmetics company in South America. Like Jessica she was once on the covers of Vogue and Time, and had even been a guest on Larry King Live. No one outside their tight circle of family

friends knew of her recluse father and her mother, a scientist with a hi-tech research facility that was completely privately funded. Kwezi and Momo always found new ways of amusing themselves with a famous picture of Isabella standing on the ruins of the orphanage she was supposed to have been raised in by nuns.

They too referred to Bella as their "mama". In Momo's case that changed when grief for her biological mother unleashed the rebellious streak that led to her untimely death. She had lived and worked closely with Bella, she's the one their mama was most proud of. They spoke a common language, united in their love for science. She was an equally dutiful daughter to her biological mother, and made regular visits to Japan, so did Hamish until his disappearance. It had pained Momo that Hamish was absent during her mother's long illness and death. Neither he nor Bella came to the funeral, and that's what left Momo wondering if her parents had ever loved or cared about anyone else outside themselves. She had stayed in Japan under the pretext of tying up her mother's loose ends; weeks turned to months and her excuses grew less convincing. She was trying to find a way out of living in her father's omnipresent shadow, and had just clinched a deal that would be the key to her freedom when she died.

Getting rid of Momo was the most difficult decision Bella had had to make after conceding to let go of Hamish many years before. She felt as broken as she was the night Hamish had told her he'd met someone that spoke to his heart. If Bella was surprised by

Hamish's decision to leave her, she did a good job in hiding her feelings. She had taken the rejection in her stride and cooked up the right story for their small circle of friends. They lapped up the tale of Hamish's decision to eschew his worldly activities in search of god and redemption.

"So where is Hamish?" I asked.

Sammy shrugged, "no one knows where he is at the moment, but we know that he's in South-Africa." He took a long sip of his drink, "I'm afraid that's all I can tell you for now, and I want to stress that we all need each other to put this to bed." The agreement was unanimous; all we needed was a plan and nerves of steel. Rosemary, Jamie and Jessica would vanish into the underbrush for a few weeks while the rest of us stuck our bleeding necks out in shark infested waters. Sammy and Jessica were tight lipped about what they had up their mutual sleeve; they wanted to leave nothing to chance and a slip of a tongue. The rest of us were simply charged with following Sammy's instructions to the letter.

A few days later he picked Eve and me up at the crack of dawn for an excursion to our mother's planet. We were already on our second cup of coffee and raw nerves when the buzzer went off. We shot out of the house dodging a barrage of questions we could not answer honestly. It was okay for Eve, since she could lie to a mind reader and get away with it; I on the other hand was sweating buckets of the hard booze I've been consuming copious amounts of since Eve moved in with me. I sank into the comfort of the sound proof, armour plated, chauffeured sedan; safe from Alana's questions and koeksisters. She cut a ridiculous figure running after the car waving a plastic container full of koeksisters. Eve and I squealed with glee and Sammy brayed, completing the theme of our menagerie on wheels. Alana's sprint set the mood for the drive to Johannesburg. Sammy kept us entertained with snippets of his colourful past in the liberation movement until we turned into Harrow road. The atmosphere took a more sombre turn when he gave us a guided tour of Kwezi's haunts and joints.

She owned a small club that doubled as an escort agency that catered for influential men and women with exotic appetites and habits. It was tucked away in a quiet street of small apartment buildings and nice Jewish family
homes. Kwezi's private club posed as one of the grander homes in the area. We drove past it slowly taking in every detail of the house that was built by a prospector who had struck gold. Our next stop was her residence in a gated neighbourhood in Houghton; the guard waved Sammy's car through without the slightest hint of hesitation.

"I own a specialised security company that provides protection for this neighbourhood." He explained, wiping the question marks off our faces, and then he said, "We'll go to her club later on."

Eve's eyes popped out and I sucked on my thumb. Sammy assured us that Kwezi wouldn't recognise us.

"Ceillidh, we'll get u brown contact lenses; this

woman hasn't laid eyes on you since the day you were born, and the last time she saw Eve she was just a fertilised embryo," he pointed out dryly.
We had late lunch in the garden of his home in Killarney. The meal and the smell of lavender had me in a peaceful state of suspended animation until it was time to play Mata Hari. The contact lenses took some getting used to but were worth every itch and scratch.

Nothing could ease my anxiety about meeting the woman I had spent all my life missing, it grew as we neared the club. Sammy stuck a card in a hole in the wall and the gate rolled open as if by magic. The cobbled driveway could easily accommodate ten Sedans comfortably, and her backyard was a pool area with a thatch-canopied bar which wrapped itself around the oval pool creating an illusion of intimacy. Once inside the pool area, the world outside slipped away.

A prime pick of elegantly turned out young women mingled with an assortment of middle aged men, most of whom had paunches; we were underdressed in our jeans and t-shirts. Eve was wearing squash shoes, an orange vintage Adidas sweater and 501s that hung loosely on her boyish frame. I had on the same jeans tucked into turquoise leather cowboy boots and a cream poncho with a random pattern of colourful, hand embroidered butterflies. It was a classic Thummie creation that was made with manic genius and a lot of love.

"Looks like we've made quite an impression," Eve spoke through a smile, her eyes were fixed on the lean man that was already making his way towards us.

"Sammy, it's good to see you again; may I see you in private?" he said, and then proceeded to shower us with compliments before slipping away with our host.

We sipped on champagne spritzers having inane conversation to kill time and the space between us and the regulars. Something was slightly off about the scene. The girls clothing didn't leave much to the imagination, and there was a primal competitive air as they milled around battling each other for the alpha female spotlight.

"I wonder what the prize is?" I said, unable to conceal my own curiosity.

"It's you ladies that are causing a stir; I've never seen my butterflies so restless. There's definitely something about the two of you." We both spun around to see the person attached to the honey laced husky voice. I was dumb struck by her presence. My mother was in my face for the first time in twenty-six years.

Eve looked her over openly, intently, "I hope that's not part of your recruitment dance because we are not on the market for work." She said.

Kwezi laughed heartily and replied, "Oh no dear child, I'd need to spend more time with you before I even consider turning you into a butterfly. It takes a special kind of girl."

Eve threw her head back laughing, "You must have stuffed up your last selection because these butterflies think they are cabbage moths," she replied. I gulped down the rest of my drink and started to retreat to the bar, away from the heat. Just then my mind leapt into action, churning out scenarios of how pear shaped things could go if Kwezi got the slightest whiff of our true identity. I doubled back and slid between them, "My partner can be a handful sometimes" I said. "My name is Ceillidh," I added with a big fat lie of a smile.

"So what do you do Ceillidh, and what are you doing in South Africa?" she asked.

I chuckled, "I'm filming a fly on the wall documentary series on foreign students working in a country hotel in Parys." I lied.

She giggled like a schoolgirl that had taken far too much whiskey and an equal amount of cigarettes. "I can't believe the things that pass for entertainment these days." She said.

"I'd drink to that," I replied waving my empty hands.

"How rude of me; I'm closing down your tab; drinks are on the house." She shrieked in a stage whisper.

"Your drinks ladies," Sammy cut in just in time to rein his daughter in. He handed me my drink; Eve stood beside him looking on sulkily, confused.

"I was just telling eh..." I started saying to Sammy.

"Ella" he said.

I smiled sheepishly and continued, "I was telling her about the reality show on the foreign students working in a Parys hotel." Eve and Sammy shared a look.

"I'm sure she'd love to come by and see it for herself," said Eve.

I could almost see the wheels in Sammy's brain turning when he said, "that can be arranged." I knew for sure that he was not talking about giving Ella a lift to Parys.

"How does a security expert get mixed up with entertainment industry types?" she asked staring directly into the centres of my eyes.

I eased them out of an instant of discomfort into an easy smile. "Sammy's security and logistical services are invaluable. He was highly recommended by a dear friend of my production manager, Eve." I jerked my head towards Eve, who accepted her new career with another chuckle. Ella excused herself and hurried away.

"Once you start you just can't stop, can you?" Eve was laughing her gorgeous head off.

"Would you rather just blurt everything out and risk finding out nothing?" I hissed. She inched closer to Sammy, already taking advantage of the perks of having a powerhouse for a father. "I hope you don't

think that he can stop me from cracking open that empty cooler box you call a head!"
They laughed, just as well because our hostess was watching us from the other end of the pool, feigning interest in whatever the man with fat rolls for a neck was saying.

"She *will* come to Parys you know?" Sammy told us. We both nodded vigorously.

"So what do we do now?" Eve asked.

"I'll organise the equipment and crew; you two just act like you know what you're doing." He looked pleased with himself.
 At least I knew a lot about film from two years of on-set catering all over England. Sometime the crews were so small, I would end up as an unwilling intern and eventually an apt Jill of all trades. I had toyed with the idea of studying film, but the erratic personalities of cocaine addicts under pressure drove me to the self-contained madness of the restaurant kitchen.

"That man she's talking to is Dwight Mohlala, the former trade unionist cum agitator turned major player in anything that makes the sun rise and set on this country." Sammy was telling Eve about the man with a meat-roll for a neck while I was between worlds. "He served a purpose for both sides, brought a means to an end, and became the embodiment of political and economic transformation. Now he's just a fat pervert with the kind of power that makes girls like these forget about the size of his podgy hips." We sniggered like a bunch of fishwives, turning more heads in the process.

We had another round of drinks and chatted to Ella for a bit longer while Sammy was making a phone call in his car. On the way back to Parys he explained that he had to make the necessary arrangements to make our imaginary film, and my imaginary film company a reality.

**Chapter 14**

I was only too grateful to curl up under the covers with a lavender flavoured thumb in my mouth. I could hear Eve and her father chatting away as I drifted in and out of sleep, yet I was still surprised to find a dishevelled Sammy having coffee in my kitchen the next morning. He asked me to sit down and said, "Just keeping up appearances, I'm afraid I had to give Ella the idea that you and I are together."

I pulled a face and made retching noises, "great now I'm fucking my half-sister's dad. No offence, but I'll never recover if I ever have to kiss you."

"I wouldn't let it come to that." He replied.

"That's a relief." I said as I scooped my keys off the table. I pecked him on the cheek, "I really must go; have a safe drive." I could sense him watching me until I was hidden by the trees. I had no delusions about the reception I would get from Alana. I knew her well enough to expect her to be nursing a grudge over us leaving without her koeksisters. True to my gut's rumblings Alana made the day seem like life in an Anglo-Boer war concentration camp for everyone.

"I want to run away to Joburg and never come back here," Justina muttered under her breath after she had taken more unsolicited abuse from Alana.

Lucia's sentiments were more malevolent, "I swear I'll murder that evil hamster of a woman as soon as lunch service is over." She had threatened.

I asked her to do it quietly in case there are little Alana clones on standby in the antique cist she would not let anyone but Abe sit on. Eve was safe in her station behind the bar, mixing and pouring drinks for a group of tourists and the regular mixed bag of farmers and trendy types. Abe was on floor manager duty, he was abusing his power to keep himself out of the kitchen and away from Alana's acid tongue. We were all guilty of being insensitive to her fears and deeply ingrained habits, especially me.

"I thought they'd never leave," Eve breathed a sigh of relief when the tourist group left some time after 5pm. We had no dinner reservations so I asked Abe to lock the gate and turn the sign to "Fully Booked".

"Why did we lock up so early today?" Alana gnashed a tune with her false teeth.

I frantically paged through the blank pages of my mind for words. There was absolute silence in the conservatory, except for the occasional sound of a greedy gulp and the suckling noises Lucia makes when drinking. I had given everyone permission to mix themselves a pitcher of their favourite cocktail, and they had gone to town on the spirits. Even Abe switched from his usual virgin to potent strawberry daiquiri; the mood was intense.

"Some of you may choose to leave after you hear what I'm about to tell you. Whether you decide to stay or abandon ship, I'd like to stress how important it is that what I tell you stays within these walls." My voice sounded dry and distant. I faltered but managed to sustain an erratic cadence until I had told them everything.  My breathing was laboured, at the end I felt like I had been running a marathon.

"I'll help you," said Abe. He was the first to swear his loyalty despite the dangers that would come with the deception I had asked them to be part of.

"You don't abandon your family in their time of need," Alana's voice was gentle but firm, it felt like the hug I sorely needed.

"Your mother is a bitch, evil!" Lucia exclaimed.

Justina nodded vigorously; she had lost her voice and her eyes were filling with tears. My sister grinned from ear to ear relieved that the worst of our fears had not come true. Sammy had warned us about not being selective with the truth, "these people don't owe you anything, you can't just put your lives in their hands?" he had said. I relished the prospect of showing him how wrong he was about the depth of the bond between strangers that had learnt to co-exist.

"This is very exciting," Justina thrilled, having recovered from paralysis.

"Does anyone else feel like eating leftover cottage pie?" Eve led the way to the kitchen, oblivious to everything else but the urgent pangs in her belly.

"You two must thank god you weren't raised by such a cold woman, you'd be totally different people." Said Alana, her words cut deep but thinking of my childhood with Angel in the wild coast, and then life with Jessica in Garelochhead put a faint smile on my face.

"I still can't find the words to tell my mother how much I appreciate her for giving up her dreams and her family so she could raise me." Eve's loud thought was muffled by the pie and chips in her mouth.

"I guess she didn't bother teaching you table etiquette," Justina observed, horrified by the contents of Eve's mouth.

"Does Koos' disappearance have anything to do with your mother?" Abe's question threw us into a loaded moment of silence.

I flicked a stray strand of hair back to its place, "I haven't thought about it that way, but now that you're bringing it up I can't help but wonder."

Alana and Eve picked up their forks and resumed eating with gusto. "Okay, what do you two know that the rest of us don't know?" Justina glared at them using her knife as a conductor's baton. They continued shovelling food into their mouths with heads bowed like competitors at an eating contest.

"Will one of you just tell the rest of us what the hell is going on here?" I banged on the table rattling the plates to get their full attention.
They exchange meaningful glances, and then Alana fished a piece of paper out of the back pocket of her khaki shorts. She laid a neatly folded telegram on the

table and slid it towards me.

"So Koos is in Hermanus, and you fools decided that it's infinitely better to keep us all in the dark about it," I scolded them. They had another quick visual chat, ignoring me. I was flabbergasted.

"When did you two become co-conspirators?" Lucia interrogated them, eyeing them suspiciously. She shook her head to communicate her disappointment at Alana's crime of sharing a secret with Eve, who had become their mutual weapon against Justina.

Alana was quick to apologise, "I'm sorry Lucia, she brought the telegram to me, and I swore her to secrecy. I may not like what Koos turned out to be, but I don't want him to go to prison either." She looked ashamed.

Abe and Justina tried to reassure her that she has done nothing wrong. Lucia nodded in agreement but would not let the offenders off the hook. "I always take in the mail, and I have never seen a telegram addressed to Alana. Where did you get that telegram?" she frowned. Alana explained that telegrams can be delivered even after the morning mail has arrived, but Lucia was not having it- "I know that; you think I'm stupid or what? I want to know how come no one else saw or heard the postman." She persisted like a wasp trying to find its way out of an empty juice bottle.

Eve shrugged and continued eating, driving Lucia off her missile-armed rocker. I excused myself, and I went to soak in bubble bath until I looked like an oversized prune with a massive shocking pink plastic head. The hideous recycled plastic shower-cap was a token of Justina's gratitude for the trip to Johannesburg.

Everyone else found their own way to settle down emotionally over the two weeks that followed, but I remained wary. I was still haunted by the fact that I knew as little about Sammy's plan as the people I had requested to trust me with their lives. He had been out of the country for almost a week and I hadn't heard a peep from him since. After the day of the family meeting, he took to contacting Eve via a handset he had bought for her. He could have been reading her French vogue at bedtime over the phone, and I wouldn't have known anything about it.

"My dad will be here in time for supper," she said as we picked broad beans and baby carrots for our evening meal.

"Dad; what caused the change of heart?" I asked, putting down the basket I was about to take to the hotel kitchen.

She looked up from the bush of beans she was picking smiling wickedly. "Their love for me is an ego kick." She said.

I could only join in the laughter when she started braying like an asphyxiating donkey, care free under the wintry sky. The evening air had grown chillier and the sun set earlier than it had a few weeks before.

"We must hurry inside before we catch a cold," I said when I noticed that her bare shoulders had broken into goose pimples.

"Aren't you supposed to be the closest thing to a black Eskimo?" she said, taunting me with her big brown eyes.

"It's you I'm worried about; this feels like spring weather to me." I replied. Part of my mind had wandered off to my parents and our beautiful home overlooking the nuclear submarine base.

"Hey, sputnik; come back to base," her smile was a star shining just for me in the stillness of the back garden.

That night we all pitched in on making supper, which was the most fun we'd had together in a long time. It felt good to have a normal conversation with the usual amount of rib digging and joy. Lucia's sardines were delicious, and we all agreed on that.

 Abe, Alana and Justina made a beeline for the door when the buzzer went off. "You two can do the dishes, we are going to have dessert on your deck and watch the stars." Alana winked at me as she closed the door.

Eve had already left the room to let daddy in. I hung back to wash the dirty dishes and warm his plate up so they could have time to catch up over a drink in the conservatory. Thomas was on my mind; I had not seen or heard from him since the day of the family meeting and I worried everyday about him being the most exposed out of all of us. I voiced out my fears for my father's safety as soon as Sammy had pushed his empty plate away.

"Tom had been in worse situations than this, he knows how to take care of himself." He said. He sounded convincing but I needed more than my father's resume for my fears to go to sleep.

My voice was shrill with impatience when I said, "I don't want to know what he's capable of; I want to know exactly where he is."

He raised a hand to calm me down, and motioned for permission to light a cigarette. I responded by getting my own box out of the breast pocket of my dungarees. He reached over to light me up before lighting his own and then he explained; without fail my jaw dropped like it was prone to whenever he was around. It turned out I was Thomas' first and only fare. When he was not wearing a beer belly and woolly beard, he was known as Sizwe "Tom" Mahlaba, the media mogul."

I did not know whether to jump for joy or cry, "my father is the eccentric idiot that gets chauffeured around in a yellow cab by an Indian woman in a purple sari." I exclaimed.

"What's with the cab?' Eve giggled. The true identity of my father was a spring of eternal mirth for her. It would have been funny for me too had I been given a fair chance to digest the news. It was common knowledge that the man had his name stencilled on every piece of linen, crockery and cutlery in all his houses. My only consolation was that he would be safe from Ella behind his dowdy taxi driver facade.

"Tomorrow we'd like to fit the house with cameras. Tom has arranged everything; he'll come talk you through the knobs and monitors." Sammy's voice trailed away towards the end, probably because his eyes were fixed on Eve. I wished that Jamie or Thomas had been there. I could do with being someone's little girl, being everyone's superwoman was taking its toll on me and on Alana, who had taken it upon herself to be my safety net.

"Did Eve tell you about the telegram Koos sent to Alana?" the words just tumbled out of my mouth on their own accord; my mind was elsewhere.

He cleared his throat, "it's nothing to worry about; the further away he is the better." He changed the subject to the more urgent affairs of preparing for Ella's looming visit. "She's really interested in you; my contact says she has a business proposition for you." He said.

My head started throbbing; I was processing all the nefarious business opportunities a woman like Ella may have for film types that are drawn to her world.

Eve tugged at the sleeve of his sports jacket, "What did you say to her?" she asked with a hint of indignation.

He had an amused look on his face when he replied, "I told her that Ceillidh is my girlfriend, and that you are her new best friend; she thinks it's a cute set-up." He giggled, revealing a perfect set of tiny gleaming teeth.

Eve looked like she was about to let go of a jet of projectile vomit. I was just too stunned by the bodies that were dropping on my bed without invitation, devoid of words to describe the maelstrom of emotions brought about by the incestuous turn in my fictitious love life. I suckled the rest of my drink the way Lucia does. "Besides our Greek love lives, what else did you say to her to make her so keen on us?" I asked.

The laughter in his face was replaced by a more serious expression. "Kwezi takes pleasure in what would make other people cringe; she actually enjoys watching the videos she uses to blackmail her clients into doing her bidding. She thinks she's finally found a way to get to me through you."

I rolled my eyes skywards, "so Eve and me are supposed to be a double-edged honey trap?" My head hung, weighed down by more deceit. "You don't expect me to cosy up to you in public do you?" I asked, horrified at the prospect.

"No, it's not my style and Ella knows that. We played her perfectly the first time around." He coughed.

"What?" I asked.

Had his skin been lighter, his face would have turned red. "Please fix a room for my driver. I can sleep in your couch again if you don't mind."

It was an unexpected request, "Okay." I replied, dragging the first syllable to emphasise my mixed feelings.

"Thanks, I'll' get my things." He got up, and left me glaring at an empty chair.

"Fix a plate for the driver and show him to room 10, I'm turning in." I told Eve, who made a face and followed me until the kitchen.

I was too drained to say anything else to her so I just left her there; I needed all my energy to kick the invaders out of my cottage so I could practice pretending that I was alone. They milled out happily skipping and hopping down the cobbled path; drunk and noisy but pleasantly malleable. I took a quick shower, and escaped to my bed with nothing else on but earplugs and a woollen beanie. When I woke up I found no one in the living room; in fact there was not a single soul in the house yet I felt like I was at the centre of a hive. I jogged down the path unable to contain the burst of energy that was driving me. It felt like I was in a dream, things were happening at warp speed but my mind was still. Tom started walking me through what was happening the moment I tumbled into the kitchen, breathless from my impulsive sprint.

Thomas was haranguing some white boys into action. "Four cameras in the kitchen, two in the hallway, four in the dining lounge, two in the conservatory, two in the upstairs hallway, two in each room, and 1 in each of the bathrooms." Thomas pointed as he spoke; his words came out like a volley of fire from a well-oiled AK-47 in capable hands. There were about half a dozen efficient technicians wiring the hotel, looking business-like in their industry uniform of khaki cargo pants. Tom pointed and spoke and I followed him in a daze. My body matched his speed but my mind was paralysed. When he was done giving me a tour of my hotel, he led me outside to the OB van that was parked all the way up the driveway.

"Where are my suppliers' delivery vans going to park? What about my regulars?" I asked. My mind had finally come alive to find the weird version of my father barking at me in clipped sentences. Panic surged through my body when the implications of the ruse finally came home to roost.

"If anything this will boost your business. We've been running an ad campaign for Hotel Parys for the past three weeks. We have at least one celebrity guest booked in for each week of the eight weeks of shooting." He rattled on, pausing only to shoo a ladybird off his sleeve. My head was spinning, and the only thing I could hold on to was the mad man that had taken over my life while I was sleeping. He was unstoppable; "We've had to close the booking hotline; we were booked solid for all eight weeks within two days of the campaign launch. You have several interviews over the next few days, and you've declined to do any more than the ones we've already confirmed. Tasha will brief you; she's my assistant, but now she's ours because I'm your production partner and we enjoy working together." He smiled broadly, and I felt myself slipping into a tiny crevice in the ground. "Great! Let's get this party started." He exclaimed. I jumped back expecting him to howl and click his heels.

"What am I doing?" I thought to myself, as I trailed two steps behind him hoping that the earth would swallow me up. The man was hopping mad, and I had the mixed blessing of being his only child; the apple of his eye, or so he claimed.

I couldn't believe my eyes when we stepped into the back of the truck. It was full of monitors and a desk with knobs, buttons, switches and four twitchy looking young men staring into screens some of whom were already transmitting audio-visual feed from my hotel. "What the fuck?" I exclaimed like a fool on idiot pills. I sunk into an empty leather swivel chair next to a very tall, very skinny girl with pillar-box red Shelley Temple curls and a puffy face that was covered in tiny, pink, stress zits.

She stuck out a long, pale hand, "I'm Tasha. Here's the folder with everything Tom said you'd want. I'm sure I've done a good job; if I haven't Tom will fire me." She spoke with the same frenetic energy that seemed to have possessed my dad. I avoided her piercing gaze and took the folder that was on the desk, ignoring the hand that was still lingering in the small space between us. "It's nice to meet you too," she said with absolutely no sarcasm in her syrupy sweet voice. I couldn't wait to get out and gasp for air; I bolted with the file without a single backwards glance.

**Chapter 15**

## The beginning of the end

Tom knew that he would find me sitting on our bench in the greenhouse. "I'm sorry about lying to you all this time," he said as he settled down beside me.

"Let me guess; I must understand because it was for my own good." I spoke softly, too tired to express the rage that was welling up inside me. He reiterated the same speech Sammy had given, but all that poured out of his mouth was even more lies and betrayal. "You should have told me the truth the moment you picked me up from the airport." I started sobbing, but thought better of it.

He hesitated before replying, "Maybe you are right, but what's done is done." He said.

"Where is Koos?" I asked; my eyes found his, daring him to lie to me again.

"He's fine; Sammy is keeping him somewhere for reasons known only to him. My priority is keeping you safe, everything else is up to Sammy and Jessica; they've always loved the intrigue." he replied. He sounded irritated and tired.

"Who are you now? Who will you be after the tree hugging media mogul has done his bit to save me from your psycho ex-girlfriend?" I asked him.

He winced at the bitter sound of my voice, and then he tried to reach out to me, but I inched away from his attempt to console me. I could not allow him to draw me into his arms, having developed prickliness to being smothered by good intentions. He displayed his unease by shifting about in his seat as if his pants were infested by flesh-eating ants. He cleared his throat to speak, and I steeled myself for more untruths.

"I'm the one who made sure that your grandfather's ship didn't sail away with you in it. I know that doesn't mean much to you right now, but I still wouldn't think twice if I had to do everything I've done to protect you." I fought back the tears, feeling like I owed the world my existence. "I was number five on the security branch's terrorist list when I smuggled myself into the country to get you out of Pondoland. I'm not claiming to be super-dad, I just want you to realise that I've always been around but unable to reach out to you."

I kept still and let him cry away his regrets and the sad memories that accompanied them. Only when his well of tears had run dry did he take out a hemp hanky so he could put himself together. I watched with naked amusement as he wiped, dusted, and blew out the evidence of his emotional outburst.

"Where was I?" He said, and then he got on with the mammoth task of explaining why he had spent most of his time in the United Kingdom even after liberation. I listened patiently as he drew me a graphic picture of why Kwezi had to believe that I had died when I was reaped out of her body. I understood because I had met my mother. Seeing the sorrowful face he kept hidden under various masks renewed my determination to help him lay his ghosts to rest.

"So in all these years you still haven't figured out what she wants from me?" I asked, not expecting an answer.

He stared into space for a while just concentrating on his breathing. "She's the director of a family owned medical and bio-technology research empire, one of the most powerful individuals in the world. It doesn't take a rocket scientist conspiracy theorist to assume that you and your sister are probably..." he paused and scratched his head.

"You can say it you know. To be honest, I just hope Eve and I are not some highly infectious disease that will wipe out most human life." I interrupted defensively.

His raucous laughter filled the greenhouse, "It's nothing that sinister but it's important enough to make your mother reduce herself to a local society figure when she could be going mad somewhere more exotically lawless." His eyes blackened with antipathy when he spoke about her.

"What made you fall in love with her?" I asked, bracing myself for romance only to be slapped in the face with a block of ice.

He took both my hands in his and spoke to me like one would to get important information through a child's head. "I honestly don't remember. What I do know is that I had a hard time remembering who I was before I let her ruin my life." He answered;

squeezing his eyes shut to clear his head like I would do when frustrated.

"Do we have time for me to make you an omelette," I asked.

His grin said it all, so we floated to the cottage with our arms linked. In the back of my mind I was churning out more questions from the answers Thomas had tried to give. Like how I had survived twenty-six years without my biological mother being the wiser, or what had spooked Angel to suicide if not Hamish's reappearance? The circus in the hotel was the furthest thing from my mind as I ambled on alongside my dad, dreaming up an omelette fit for a famished king and his giant princess.

The time we'd spent talking and dining was the longest we had been in each other's company since the day ensnaring Kwezi and Hamish took over our lives. It had only been three days since we had started streaming twenty-four hours of live content from the hotel on Tom's satellite channel. He also beamed free footage to any other channel that had wanted it; only a few turned him down.

The overwhelming response from the public turned Justina, Abe, Lucia and Alana into international celebrities overnight. I on the other hand had been replaced by a midnight blue block of an efficient dyke with a crew cut, and a shiny pair of square-toed boots. The staff called her Amin, although they were quite aware that her name was Mina.

I was invited to every talk show in the country, but Tasha declined all appearances on my behalf citing a tight schedule as an excuse. She packaged pre-recorded interviews, which comprised of me perjuring myself repeatedly for different target-audiences.

Truth be told, all I did was swivel about on the chair munching on energy bars in the OB van. Tasha insisted on doing everything else in her zeal to impress me, an impostor. I was so bored I had even lost interest in the monitors and their twenty-four hours stream of banality. Each day I woke up more sickened by the streams of young women and pre-pubescent girls that were choking up the road screaming Abe's name, but on that particular day I was thankful to them for the purpose they had given to my life.

Since Tom was the self-appointed creative, he decided it was fair to leave all the buttering up of irate town's officials to Sammy and me. We left the hotel grounds armed with figures and Sammy's sweet tongue. It was his company that paid the neighbouring farmers a king's ransom to allow his security men to be deployed on their land. He had also covered the city's costs for providing police support at check points. He was the de facto chief in town; the town's men were all over him like crush-stricken cheer leaders. Not only was he a bottomless purse, he was also a struggle hero with impeccable credentials. His presence paved the way to a swift and painless meeting. We had jointly worked out a plan to keep the fan traffic in town, but out of the roads and away from the hotel.

My phone rang while he was presenting that plan. I apologised, switched the phone off, and scribbled a mental note to return the call to the unfamiliar number that was still flashing in my mind's eye.

All that was left was for me to do was talk about Tasha's plan to direct business to the city's establishments, "making Parys the hippest place to be," as she had proclaimed. I could see the wads of cash piling up in the city officials' eyes, and realised we were walking on water. It didn't take a savant to grasp that the spell would last for as long as the money continued to flow into the right hands.

"You know that there'll still be potholes in this town a year from now right?" Sammy said once we were in his car.

I giggled, "I could see them contemplating whether to import something rare and Italian, or to settle for the most expensive German model on the market." I replied. I had already grown accustomed to health inspectors that would propose to neglect their duties if they could pop-in for free meals with friends and family. I always turned down such propositions, but I had been tempted to slip a traffic officer his "cool drink" to avoid an unnecessary delay whose sole purpose was extortion. Corrupt officials seemed to outnumber the hands that filled their pockets, and I had accepted that as a fact of life. "At least there'll be more jobs and interest from Tasha types that will make the buzz work for them." I observed dryly, looking out into the rain. "So, you are willing to change the face of an entire town just to get at my mother." I added, looking as sullen as I sounded.

I waited in vain for an answer, but instead he poured me a finger of whisky in a crystal glass and then proposed a toast to the future. I downed the drink and gestured at him to pour me another.

"The future: my arse." I said. I'd had enough of the control freak and his elaborate pranks. "I think I'll take my chances on my own. I like the way things were before you gate crashed my life. I want your freak show out of my property, or I'll have you arrested for fraud and for kidnapping Koos."

He raised an eyebrow and poured me three fingers more than before in a clean glass.

"Christ, you've murdered him haven't you?" I said.

He laughed. "'That's not the worst thing I could do to him; if that was the case, he would have died painfully many years ago." I believed him.

"I can't do this if you all keep telling me half-truths." I whinged intent on squeezing the stone until it yielded water.

He rolled his eyes in resignation and replied, "I think you and I should take a drive to Johannesburg." He spoke to his driver through the intercom, and the car turned around.

"I guess this is the only way," I muttered sulkily, but inside I was having a farewell party to Parys.

The celebration was rather short-lived because the more I learned about Kwezi along the way, was the less festive the mood of the private party in my head. I was totally unprepared for the fact that while I was doggy paddling in a rock pool in Port St John's, Kwezi was bargaining with repressive governments for human guinea pigs that were selected from lists of prisoners and political "undesirables". Until then I believed I had come to terms with Kwezi's propensity for evil-doing. But the truth and what I believed were separated by a mountain of dark secrets that was embodied by my loved ones, who seemed bent on shining the light away from veracity. I was up to my ears in their noble intentions, so I took Sammy's lust for vengeance prisoner and tortured it to get the facts out of him.

She was five months pregnant with me when she went underground. That was after her people had tipped her off that the Liberation Movement had taken an unhealthy interest in her. At the time Tom felt that it would have been better if she had been kidnapped by the security police and tortured as he'd first suspected. He had already invested too much of his heart in her when allegations of her nefarious activities came to light. According to his comrades' reports, she embodied the evil he was fighting against, and she was about to give birth to his child.

"Thomas has always been a sentimental fool," Sammy stated his observation as a matter of fact. I responded by raising an eyebrow, biting my tongue so he could tell me more.

When Kwezi was spotted in the Seychelles Tom had begged Sammy to let him save his unborn child. Sammy was his commander and best friend; he couldn't refuse Tom a chance to rectify his mistake.

There were no courts in their world; justice was metered out by assassination. It was up to Tom and his conscience to make things right, but Sammy wondered how he would go about taking the life of the woman he'd adored and save the child that was inside her.

"Dead people don't need anaesthetic for a Caesarean." Tom had quipped. All Sammy could do was hope that he would never get to experience what his friend had been through.

Tom made it safely to the Seychelles and took over from the comrade who had been watching her. He kept track of her every move for a few more days waiting for the right opportunity to strike. That time came when she set out for a jaunt on her boat; a momentary lapse of judgement that was brought about by her passion for sailing.

Tom stowed away in the boat's shower and took over the vessel when land was out of sight. She didn't know what happened, one moment she was staring into the open sea and then there was blackness. She didn't feel Tom and his German companion carry her into a speedboat, nor did she see her Leila sink soundlessly. They had changed course towards Tanzania where the German's ship was waiting for its human cargo. They set sail for Cape Town leaving Kwezi on a life raft off the coast of Somalia.

She was meant to be picked up by friends of the liberation movement, but jungle-justice was foiled by the tracking device that was embedded in her calf. Her people got to her first, but her enemies were left to assume that she had fallen into the hands of pirates when the bullet-riddled, blood-splattered raft was found five nautical miles south of where she had been left floating. Her life had been spared but she had lost her child, and her ability to carry another to full term.

Tom and the German parted ways in Cape Town; neither the German nor his ship was ever seen again. Tom disembarked as an Indian trader from Kenya and went straight to Athlone. He left Cape Town two days later as a young nun accompanying an orphaned infant to her late parents' relative. He had all the relevant credentials in his possession, and a letter from a convent in Natal to the child's guardians. A real priest picked him up at the train station in Cape Town and drove him to the Eastern Cape.

"If you people want her dead, why don't you just make her dead? You've been great at making things happen so far by the sound of things," I reached for the bottle that was resting in its customised indent on the retractable table between us.

"I would give up my life to save hers; that's how important she is to us." He replied.

A chill settled at the bottom of my stomach in spite of the hot liquid I kept pouring down my throat. I encouraged him to carry on.

"Is your phone still switched off?" he asked.

The question annoyed me but I looked for it in my bag and switched it on. I returned the last call; the voice on the other end was familiar but I still could not put a face to it, "Its Ella darling," she sounded neither excited nor bored.

I forced a telephone smile, "did you get my number from Sammy?" I asked, glowering at him.

"Oh, no darling, my PA does the fetching. I want to have lunch with you next week."

I told her that I had a busy schedule, but she could be my guest on set in the next week. She said she'd chew on it and ring me back. "Why don't I come by to your club for a quick drink, I'm less than an hour away." I replied. At which point Sammy grinned like the Cheshire cat that swallowed all the mice in Hamlin.

"Brilliant, I'll see you then." She replied, and then she hung up.

I looked at Sammy with renewed suspicion, "if she is who you say she is; what is she doing in Yeoville playing pimp for goons in suits?" I asked.

He ran his hands over his clean shaven head and rolled his eyes, "you must have bumped your head countless times over the past few days because I know you are not that stupid." He exclaimed in disbelief. "Ella's club is her African power base, the offices in Sandton is where she keeps her corporate staff. This woman runs a multi-national from her palm pilot." He sighed and made an elaborate show of taking a sip from his glass. "Just keep your eyes and ears open; you'll see for yourself." he added patiently, smiling like the Sammy I was growing fond of.

We were ushered in by a maid; Ella was in the club's kitchen preparing Thai prawn curry for lunch. She looked beautiful in a flowing white linen dress that outlined her slender frame when she walked. Her blue eyes slanted upwards under thick black eyelashes. Her eyes were considerably smaller than mine and oriental, but the distinct blue was exactly like mine and Jessica's. She had her thick, black curls cropped into an afro which made an ideal frame for her almost too wide lips and high cheekbones set on a flawless olive complexioned canvas. Even her earlobes looked perfect dressed in small platinum studs with blue diamond gumdrops dangling off single strands of platinum string.

She smiled broadly, and greeted us by showing us to the already set table at the centre of the kitchen. I made myself comfortable and exchanged pleasantries with her while Sammy uncorked the champagne that was already in the ice bucket. He poured two glasses and served me and Ella before sitting down to pour his own.

"What's the occasion?" I asked.

"I thought you liked a good champagne-spritzer, or was that an occasion?" She replied.

I laughed heartily, like I used to at Alasdair's boring jokes. "I don't mind champagne, it's my girlfriend that can't live without it." I took a long sip savouring the strange taste of lies.

"Sammy seems serious about you; I've never seen him like this around a woman." She said, and then she tasted the sauce and turned the gas knob off.

I got up to fetch the bowl of rice off the warming plate on the kitchen counter, "I don't know about Sammy, but I'm happy with my life the way it is." I replied; I knew she was digging.

She shook her head in mock resignation saying, "young people these days; permanence scares the hell out of them."

I mixed the ingredients for Caesar salad dressing while she garnished her curry with fresh coriander and yoghurt. Sammy poured himself another drink and I went back to the chair opposite his. Lunch with Ella was pleasant; I enjoyed her company although I was aware of the limits of how low I could let my guard down. She seemed as interested in Hotel Parys as every other individual that had caught the bug. Her questions kept us going until our dessert of plump chocolate coated strawberries and more champagne. I pretended not to notice the intense, almost sexual cat and mouse game that was playing out between Ella and Sammy. Their distrust of each other had developed into a relationship that could be easily confused for a comfortable friendship.

She dusted her lips lightly with her napkin as a force of habit, and not out of necessity. "I have to go into the office, please have drinks on me." Her lips stretched into a slow smile, "I hope you'll still be here when I get back."

I glanced at my watch and replied, "I don't think we'll still be here, but you can come have lunch with me and maybe tell me more about why you wanted to see me."

She gestured for me to hang on, "Excuse me for a minute," she said.

She left the room and returned moments later carrying a small leather backpack and a palm pilot. She navigated through her diary, and asked if next Thursday would be fine.

I pressed "one" on the speed dial and Tasha's candy land voice said, "hi, Ceillidh?" within the first three rings.

I was a bit taken aback, "uh, can I fit lunch into my schedule for next Thursday?" I asked, half expecting her to laugh at me.

Instead I waited for about fifteen seconds and then she said, "You are filling in for Tom; he cannot do the sponsors' tour of the set."

I was convinced she was pulling my leg. I cleared my throat, "are you serious?" I asked.

"As a heart attack," she replied.

"Thanks, I'll see you later." I hung up. Ella made a "what now" face.

"I have to go back to the production office this evening," I lied.

"You don't seem too broken up about it," she observed.

"The hotel is my biggest priority right now," I replied truthfully.

"Next Thursday in Parys is perfect for lunch, Sammy will arrange for a car."

She started to protest, "I won't take no for an answer; standard courtesy for guests, no exceptions." I explained, thankful for Tom's famous policy of doing everything perfectly all the time.

"I really must go." she said, glancing at her watch.

Sammy stood up to hug her. I did the same, and then she ushered us out through a small private garden on the side of the house. We entered the pool area unnoticed.

"You've never been through this way, have you?" I asked him once we were alone, sitting side-by-side on the swing chair by the poolside.

"I've only seen every inch of this whorehouse through a third eye." He whispered into my ear.

His lips almost graze my earlobe. He was a sexy man but I was not about to go down the soap opera route. I would never be able to look at myself naked again, nor would Eve. "My ears are very sensitive," I stuttered.

"Jesus Christ!" he exclaimed. "Your dad will have me killed." He added in a whisper. The eldest of the three men having lunch at the table across the pool nodded a greeting, and Sammy nodded back.

"What's that about?" I asked, curious.

"We are greeting each other in a fashion most people do when they are in the middle of an important meeting."

The sarcasm did not escape me but I had a more pressing question in mind. "Who conducts business in a whorehouse?" I asked.

He jerked his head towards the three men he had just greeted. "Powerful men and women that buy and sell mines, forests, people, weapons and anything else that translates to millions of dollars. This house is the nerve centre of everything that is wrong with this country." He clenched and unclenched his fists as he spoke. "This is not the outcome I signed up for when I joined the liberation movement."

I looked at him through a fresh pair of eyes filled with new admiration. "Aren't you satisfied with having the spoils of the victors?" I asked.

He shook his head. "I do business ethically," he said. "I've never used my struggle credentials to get ahead, and I loathe people that believe that having fought their own freedom entitles them to a larger portion of the spoils than everyone else that endured the same evil."
My head bobbed for him to continue, I was

mesmerised by the flames in his eyes. "The man I greeted is Uncle Victor, he's everyone's uncle. Well at least everyone that was anyone in the liberation movement has gone through his house in Lusaka. No one knows what nationality he is but he holds great sway, which places him above the country's laws."

My skin crawled, "what does Uncle Victor do for a living when he's not slithering on his belly in hell?" I asked. We tittered; high on champagne bubbles and the concentrated wickedness in the air.

"He owns a nightclub in Hillbrow, that's the headquarters of the biggest legitimate drug syndicate. He has another nightclub in Rosebank; he calls it the meat market."
I wished he wouldn't tell me more but I had a feeling he had good reason to do so.
"Everyone else knows him for his record company, his chain of jazz clubs and his presence at every major Liberation Party event. He was at the launch party when the Liberation Movement became the Liberation Party; that was before the first democratic elections." His "comrades" cast knowing glances at us, so he put his arm around me and kissed me on the cheek to confirm their gossip.

He continued; "some say he is the benevolent granddaddy of the revolution, because his criminal activities provided a considerable amount of arms and blood-diamond money. Unfortunately some powerful elements within the LP have made sure that his illicit business profits make up a sizeable chunk of the underworld's GDP. It's easier for them to launder the money and entrench their power now that they are in power."

I felt impotent, like live bait in the path of a ravenous shoal of piranhas. "Can we talk about this somewhere less oppressive?" I asked.
He responded by helping me up and holding my hand all the way back to the car. "How do you separate your friends from your enemies?" I asked once we had driven out of the yard.

He shrugged and said, "The easiest way is by knowing how the money they have in the bank got there in the first place..." he cut himself off at the sound of my phone ringing.

"It's Tasha; it's a good thing we are heading back. Alana refuses to come out from under her bed." I said.

He threw his head back and hooted, "It looks like your pretend job is becoming a full-time occupation; I must hand it to you for handling it like a pro though." I didn't know whether he was serious or taking the piss; I said nothing.

He continued with his tale: "Uncle Victor has been Africa's number one human trafficking kingpin for a long time. When he first met Ella she was his reliable passport to Central Europe, North America and Asia. That was before you were born, when the rest of the world did not have to pretend that the wealth of the continent is more important than the people on it. People like Ella had more power than they do now; she could move across all worlds because her money and her alliances influence the price of bread and bullets in the third-world.

Her company was running secret biological-weapons research projects in South-Africa with the army, and we were their natural enemy and test subjects. The official Popular Liberation Movement resolution was to capture or kill her, but she was also an ally to powerful people in the movement. That's what made it possible for her to return with a new face and strong political connections that enabled her to reinvent her company. But now that the LP has broadened Uncle Victor's influence, she has become expendable.

Rumour has it that Uncle Victor is launching an offensive against Ella, and behind him are five of the most powerful men in the LP. They call them "The Big Five" for obvious reasons. They have their fingers in every pie that bears the "proudly South African" logo. She's in a tight spot but so are they; they are the only ones that had the dossier on Ella's true identity yet they established the ties between her and the LP regardless. We think they are planning to leak carefully sanitised information on her involvement in international human trafficking syndicates. We also know that Ella is planning on using the technical know-how she believes you can provide to leak some explosive blackmail material to prevent that from happening." He finished his story and poured us both glasses of sparkling water.

I didn't have anything to say; I had an alcohol and truth hangover. My eyes were growing heavier and it was already dark by the time we drove through the first checkpoint. I would have loved to soak in a warm bath and jump straight to bed, but Tasha had been ringing me at least once every ten minutes. I was sure I had developed an aggressive brain tumour the size of a car battery over a period of an hour and a half.

## Chapter 16

Apparently Alana had locked herself up in her room, switched the lights off and hid herself under the bed. The fishbowl life had finally gotten under her skin. The Hotel Parys website was inundated with messages from distraught fans. Things got so bad; Tom's television company had to create an emergency hotline. When we arrived Tom was standing in the middle of the driveway dressed in a sari. Tasha was pacing circles around him; he was making rude hand gestures at whoever was on the other side of the line. She stopped walking to nowhere, and started sprinting towards the car so fast the driver has to screech to a halt.

"You better handle your friend over there." I told Sammy sternly, preparing myself for Tasha who was already banging on the window.

"What the fuck is wrong with you?" I slapped her on the forehead much harder than I had intended. Her face scrunched up; I could see her deciding whether to cry or not. "Do you love your job?" I asked. She straightened up in a wink, and started walking towards the mobile office next to the OB van. I learnt that Alana was still under the bed, that the sponsors wanted cameras in the showers and above the bath, and that Tom's ex-wife kidnapped Freddy Mercury, his pet tortoise. I was stopped dead in my tracks by the force of the absurdity of the situation I had gotten Alana into.

Tasha dropped the bomb, "she's really going to boil him, the police are in Chi's house trying to talk her out of it, and Tom is talking to his life coach." I gave her the look she remembered from just before I slapped her. "She's still under the bed," she said, and then she resumed walking.

Tom spotted me and hurried down the driveway with the phone still stuck to his ear. I pushed him aside after kissing his cheek; Alana was more important to me than a boiled tortoise called Freddy Mercury. I went into the OB van; it reeked of stale weed and sweaty feet. The monitors were alive with the activity in the kitchen and the cafe, and the editing crew looked like zombies on speed. Ian the red-eyed director glanced at me nervously muttering something to his assistant, and then he gestured that we speak outside. I didn't budge; "cut off the live feed from the kitchen and Alana's room please, immediately," I said, squaring up to him.
My stiletto boots and six foot frame had me nose to nose with the "nerve-wrecking ball"; at least that's what his crew called him. He lived up to Tom's description of an efficient terrorist that exploits people's emotions and self-worth to get optimal results. He narrowed his eyes, and yelled the instructions at his assistant without breaking our staring contest.

"Great thanks. If you broadcast any footage of me entering or leaving Alana's room, I'll make sure that you spend the next five years in court." I said with a cold smile.

The room fell into a funereal silence. I could hear the consistent crunch of gravel under Tasha's pacing feet over the distant drone of the generator truck that was parked near the barn.

Ian was quietly seething, singeing my eyeballs with the fire from the centre of his. I left him standing in the middle of the silent room naked to the open stares of his crew. Tasha rushed towards me and started to say something but I gestured at her to "talk to the hand", so she just followed me until the kitchen door. She was at her wits end; the space ship was veering off course and Captain Tom was incapacitated. The whites of her eyes matched the colour of her hair, "I can only handle this one problem at a time," I said, gently shutting the kitchen door in her distressed face.

Amin was grilling line-fish, cursing the person that had the brilliant idea of "Seafood Night".

"Someone had to save this town from the generic tastes of the mass produced seafood franchise menu." Lucia replied bravely. When she saw me she dropped the scallops she was rinsing into the sink and squeezed me tight around my midriff. Her smelly hands crumpled the fitted jacket of my pant suit; "Alana started freaking out from out of the blue, she wouldn't come out of her room after her afternoon break," she cried out. Her voice was muffled by the fabric of the jacket she was creasing with her moist breath. Abe rushed in carrying four empty plates and an empty pitcher. He was relieved to see me even though I bit his head off for not leaving the pitcher in the bar.

"Jugs, bottles, cans and glasses never leave the bar area," I said, disentangling myself from Lucia's damp tentacles to give him the hug he looked like he needed.

"I needed those scallops ten minutes ago, and I want four side salads to go with this line fish right now!" Amin yelled.

Lucia raced back to her duties with renewed vigour. I gave Abe a brief squeeze when he was done tossing scraps and lining the dishes on the rinsing rack. Judging by his posture, a pep talk would do him better than marching orders. "There are only two hands in the kitchen, you and Justina need to wash some dishes as you go along." I told him as I drizzled homemade chocolate sauce on the four helpings of profiteroles he had to take to a group of "lecherous rich bitches". That's how Justina described them when she came in huffing under the weight of the three tiered silver cake platter that's used for the two course seafood "feast for four".

"They've been giving me hell since they arrived here. First they wouldn't let me serve them, now they are making stupid jokes about my Russian accent. I'm fucking Polish for fuck's sake." She ranted, violently discarding uneaten sea snails, various shells, empty exoskeletons, bones and garnish.
"I feel like shit," she moaned, banging the lid of the compost bin to illustrate how shitty she felt. "I've already ordered table three's cappuccinos at the bar, I'll get their petit fours out of the cooler," she added in a less harassed tone.

"When you are done, wash some plates and go check on the coffee." I said, preparing to start banging on Alana's door. To everyone's surprise

Alana stepped out of her room, and walked out the door with the little heart shaped basket Justina had just placed on the table.

"I'll kill that impossible dwarf if we run out of petit fours; there's only nine servings left in the fucking fridge." Amin was saying as I chased after Alana, joining Tasha who was already hot on her tail.

I caught up with them on the deck of my cottage, where Sammy was stretched out on a sun-lounger looking into the evening sky through the glass roof. We sat on the chairs around the table as quietly as humanly possible. He took one look at us and headed for the living room shutting the sliding door behind him.

"Let me tell you something," Alana's brown pointing finger jabbed in my direction as she spoke, "if you think I'm a performing seal you have one hell of a thing coming." She popped an entire ball of chocolate in her mouth.

"We had an agreement," I reminded her while her mouth was duly occupied. She raised one hand to shut me up and another shooed Tasha away. She tried to protest, but I banished her to the living room regardless.

"I don't think Sammy likes me, and besides I have some pressing matters to discuss with you," she protested, on the brink of tears.

"You either watch television with Sammy until I'm done, or you can go home and not come back; it's entirely your choice." I answered impatiently. She hurried into the cottage accompanied by Alana's wicked cackle.

She slid the heart-shaped basket towards me. "Listen liefie," she said. Her hand was dithering between taking the last chocolate and letting me have it. I snatched it and took a small bite, savouring the smoothness of the chocolate and the crunch of the pistachio nuts. "I'm still willing to do everything I can to help you, but don't expect me to show my naked bum for these ratings Ian is ranting about," she paused to suck on her brown tongue. I was dumbstruck; no one had said anything to me about nudity.
"I told him to stick the camera up his own arse," she grinned, baring her dentures in all their chocolate coated glory.

"How about you start from the beginning," I said impatiently.

"Why don't you ask that skinny red devil of an errand girl?" she spat venomously.

I told her to stay put and fetched Tasha, who was relieved that I'd come to "save her" from being ignored to death by Sammy "You have exactly thirty seconds to make sense to me," I told Tasha. Alana was still seating with her back to the door whiling time away with the rest of the confection she had half-offered me.

Tasha drew in a deep breath and then proceeded to run her mouth. "The sponsors offered us one million more per week if we work in a bit more nudity and drama. Tom was too wrapped up in Freddy Mercury's kidnap drama to be of any use to me so I decided to wait for you so we could talk about it. During lunch I told Ian that the sponsor wanted us to heat things up a notch, so we brainstormed and came up with a few ideas. I didn't expect the guy to stick cameras in the staff bathrooms. I tried to stop him when i realised he was re-rigging the place, but he threatened to quit and then Alana locked herself up in her room. As if that was not enough; Ian replaced booked guests with four floozies we now have to pay doing an appalling job at flirting with Abe." She let out a long sigh and buried her face in her hands.

I took Alana's small hand in mine and said, "The cameras in the bathrooms are coming down, Ian is fired and the sponsor can pay members of their own staff a million rand to shit and shower in public."

Alana breathed a sigh of relief, but Tasha shot upright like a lightning bolt. "That's like setting fire to twelve million rand!" she proclaimed to deaf ears; neither I nor Alana cared about the figures.

"We are sticking to the original production plan; this is a reality show not a soap opera. If the sponsors are not satisfied with the original idea Tom pitched to them, they should have raised their concerns before they signed on the dotted line." I replied.

Alana stood up, "I'll make us some tea," she said.

Tasha's lips made an "o" shape but nothing came out. "Don't say anything more about the money; I don't care. It's not about the money. Just pretend you understand where I'm coming from and you'll do just fine." I explained to Tasha while Alana was taking over my kitchen.

The worry line that runs diagonally across her forehead made another appearance, "Tom will send me to our Northern Cape office when he finds out that he lost thirty-five million under my runny nose." She said.

I laughed until my stomach hurt. "You've obviously never been to the Northern Cape; it's the nerve centre of limbo. He only opened an office there because he doesn't have the heart to fire people." She explained, gnawing frantically at her French manicure. She stopped abruptly when she realised she was ruining three hundred rand per week worth of a brief beauty salon stopover. "Great, my manicurist is going to crucify me," she cursed fluently. She raged on as if I were a priest taking her confession.

"I can't imagine life after this; there are people in the industry that would cut off their feet for the opportunity to work for Sizwe International. My only option would be to work for one of the stragglers; that's what Tom calls his competitors. Brace Media has been trying to poach me for a while now, but it would take a miracle for Sunette Meyer to be half as exciting as Tom is." She ran out of words and went back to taking her frustrations out on her nails.

"No one is sending you north of Kimberly." I assured her: I was actually thinking about the hotel and the familial bond I had formed with my staff. Their confidence in me filled me with an overwhelming amount of love. It was at that moment that the full weight of my responsibility for their safety settled on my shoulders like lead epaulets. I had to put Tasha on a more manageable page lest her panic leads to suspicion. "Tasha, I want you to listen to me very carefully because I won't repeat this," I said. "If I wanted to create smut, I would have picked a brothel instead of a hotel. Hotel Parys is my baby and Sizwe International is the paid babysitter; your duties are limited to hiring, firing and making every day run without a hitch. Anything more is you assuming authority that Tom's contract with me doesn't allow him to exercise; that will certainly get you fired and Tom sued by me." She swallowed my bluff whole and gulped down a lump of relief.

"I'll let them know that we are not accepting their offer first thing in the morning." She said.

I ruffled her hair. "That's my girl," I teased, and she cracked a wan smile. "We'll be okay after a cup of tea," I promised. That was the biggest lie I told that day.

"She murdered Freddy Mercury," Tom wailed like a child crying over a bleeding gash. He stumbled up the stairs with the agility of a deer with one broken leg; a sobbing man in a sari was too much for me to process. I left him with Tasha because she adored him enough to put up with anything he could possibly throw at her. Alana and the pot of tea she was bringing out collided with me on my way to the bedroom. She took one look at the pair outside through the sliding, and followed hot on my heels. She spent the night in my room; we talked until it

**was impossible for us to keep our eyes open without cutting out our eyelids.**

**Chapter 17**

Ella phoned me the day before our lunch date to ask for a postponement because she had to go away for two weeks. "I'll ring you as soon as I get back," she said and then hung up without saying goodbye.

Ian was gone, and in his place was a skittishly efficient slip of a woman called Martha. She was a sought after documentary filmmaker and music video director. Tasha had managed to pull her out of a hat to redeem herself in my eyes for fuck knows what.

Eve was enjoying playing production manager so much she'd forgotten she's an apathetic undergrad. She was always the first to arrive at the mobile office and the last one to leave. The research she'd done served her well enough to have Tasha wondering where she'd been all her life.

I spent most of my time having lunch with Tom, and television channel executives that wanted syndication rights.

Then there was the stream of invitations to events hosted by companies that were wooing us to take more of their money. The roller coaster ride reached its peak on the fourth week of Hotel Parys; Sammy invited me to a party he couldn't afford to attend without his new squeeze on his arm.

I was keen to see how the upper crusty lived, so I jumped at the offer.

At our arrival my jaw betrayed my reaction to the opulence of the interior. The host's banquet hall was transformed into a Monte Carlo casino. There were two roulette and two blackjack tables, six slot machines, a cafe area, a cigar lounge, three bars and three buffet tables.

The guest list included several ambassadors and the Swazi King; I mistook him for a retired basketball star that had eaten too many sweet potato pies. I knew no one, and expected to spend half the night reciting my brief script from behind Sammy's formidable shadow. It was mind boggling at first to have people ask me if I could magic an internship for their son or daughter. I must have given my number to half the people I shook hands with, all of them hoping to secure a wrap party invite for their privileged spawn.

"I thought rich people were supposed to be beyond hustling for freebies," I scoffed later that night, curled up next to him on his living room couch sipping on Horlicks out of a hideous mug.

He chuckled, "take the key and run with it my petal," he said with a cunning glint in his eyes.

I looked at him quizzically and said, "What on earth are you babbling about?"

He wiped off my Horlicks moustache, and kissed the tip of my nose, "they want what you have; take what you want." He said.
I met his gaze with a puzzled look on my hot face. It wasn't the alcohol that was giving me hot flushes; I'd only had two cosmopolitans. "I don't want anything from those people; I just want my life back." I said, earnestly yearning for a time not long ago, before I got mixed up in plotting to entrap my biological mother. What really unsettled me were the unwholesome feelings I was developing for him.

"What's bothering you, besides you wanting your life back?" he asked.

His tone assured me that he would keep the sun from rising if the promise of dawn was the cause for my unease. We talked about ourselves for the first time since we'd met, and then he asked me about my soon to be final divorce. "What's it to you'" I asked, slightly annoyed that he'd brought up vile Alasdair. He leaned closer for the kiss that could change everything between us. He wanted more than a reckless affirmation of attraction that was conveyed when our lips locked for a brief moment. I argued that he *was* old enough to be my father. He told me that if he were my father his feelings for me would make him a social deviant. We debated about how making our relationship permanent would affect Rosemary and Eve. He made it clear that if that was the only hurdle, then he'd spend the rest of his days fighting my resolve.

Facing my half-sister wasn't as difficult as I thought it would be; the hardest part was containing the euphoric state I was in. Weeks had passed but the high remained.

"What's wrong with you, are you taking drugs?" Tasha interrogated me when she caught me sitting on the deck in front of the laptop smiling at a dried fig.

"I'd be happy, but that wouldn't last," I admitted, grinning like the cat that got the cream and the tuna. I didn't have to put up a front for Tasha, "I can't wait for this production to be over, so I can get away from him."

She hooted, "So you're going to keep your crush a secret and die unfulfilled? That would suck, because the chemistry between the two of you is off the radar." she opined sardonically.
I chortled thinking about how deliciously scandalous we would all be in Tasha's eyes when she learned the truth.

"I don't want to add odd vibes to an already hectic schedule. I trust you'll keep your mouth zipped shut or risk losing your tongue," I held out my hand for her to shake.

"It's not like I have a choice; everything you say to me is confidential according to the contract I signed for this job." she grumbled, shaking my hand with enough force to dislocate my shoulder. "Do you have any idea why Sizwe is in such a foul mood lately?" she added in a stage whisper.

"I think he's still mourning for Freddy Mercury," I fibbed.

Truth be told, the show was nearing the end, but Ella had still not returned from her travels. A mood of gloom and doom hung above Tom and Sammy like a personalised storm cloud. The setback had hit them harder than the rest of us who were directly affected by Ella and Hamish. Her prolonged absence caused a flurry of clandestine activity that put a permanent furrow on Sammy's brow. Each day was an emotional pressure-cooker that was intensified by our platonic affair; I worried about his safety and lived for his phone calls. I was convinced I had either lost him or my mind when he vanished for two days. Tom was also troubled but insisted we carry on as usual.

"If anything bad happens to Sammy it won't go unnoticed, trust me," he had said, when he found me crying in the hothouse. "You are more broken up than Eve, and he's been acting weird around me since the two of you went to that ridiculously extravagant shindig; is there something I should know about?" my intuitive father had me in a tight corner, and I didn't have the energy to scheme my way out of it.

"I guess there's no point in hiding it from you; we've been-" I started to explain but he stopped me.

"I really don't want to know." He cried out, waving his hands for emphasis.

"I'm a twenty-six years old divorcee for crying out loud. I could be seeing rip van winkle and it still wouldn't be any of your business." I snapped back.

He squeezed his eyes shut with his hand and started practicing his yoga breathing exercises. "He's my best friend: you are my only child, and his daughter is half-sister. Your fling is inappropriate if not vulgar." He rationalised. "How about we go for a drive?" he suggested with a hint of a smile playing on his lips.

Ella called when we were having our second cups of

coffee and our first helping of milk tart at a home industry cafe in town.

"I'm back my dear, and I'm looking forward to that lunch you said you'd cook," she purred into my ear.

"Can you come on Sunday?" I suggested. We settled on sending a driver to pick her up at eleven, and I lied about having to be brief because of a meeting.

"Samuel will be pleased to know that we are back on track," Tom jabbered, excited.

I didn't know whether to punch him or strangle him, so I resorted to shouting at him for eavesdropping and being cagey about things I needed to know. "When the hell were you going to tell me that you have a way of contacting him?" If I had gotten angrier I would have spontaneously combusted. He left a hundred rand note on the table and literally dragged me out to the car.

"I am not getting in," I objected, furious at him for treating me like a four year old. "What is wrong with you?" I screamed at the top of my voice, which turned heads and slowed down people's pace.

He gave me a terse father to stubborn brat ultimatum: "Just get into the car, I'll explain on the way." The only reason I climbed in was so I could strangle straight answers out of him. "I honestly don't know where he is, but I would know if something was wrong," he said as he negotiated the car out of the parking space. He joined the afternoon traffic and continued, "All our numbers are linked, including yours; every call we make or receive is routed through a control room." he paused to light an incense stick that was on an incense stick holder that is a custom feature of his dashboard. "This means our positions can be triangulated at any given time, whether our phones are on or off. As for Samuel, if he doesn't check his messages every thirty minutes, his phone will send a distress signal. That's how I know he's not in trouble, so you can rest easy." He concluded his informative diatribe with three quick honks of his horn.

He turned his head to give me a beatific smile that irked me. I had to physically restrain myself from slapping him across the face with the soles of my ballet slippers. "Are you having a seizure?" he'd asked, turning into a narrow lane that was better suited for carriages.

"I'm trying very hard not to cause you any physical harm since that might get both of us killed," I answered frankly. "Why didn't I know all of this all along? I'm starting to feel like the pawn in your little game. The worst thing is I still don't see how you plan on getting Ella to confess to who she is..." I was cut off by Tom's phone ringing.

"I'll see you shortly," he said and then he hung up. "Samuel is on his way," he told me with a considerable amount of frost in his voice.

"Why is he Samuel all of a sudden?" I goaded him mercilessly.

"Nicknames seem inappropriate considering that he

may be having sex with my daughter," he replied, glowering at the road ahead.

We travelled in silence for the rest of the way, and remained stone-faced when the valet waved us to the production crew parking space. Tasha had also hired two ushers and two usherettes to help keep the guests within the velvet rope and away from the grounds. Thomas parked his cab in his spot right next to the mobile office in the make-shift reserved parking bay. I went straight to the office to check in on Eve, but Thomas popped his head in a few minutes later. "Ceillidh, please come with me," he said; Eve and I exchanged looks.

Tasha expressed her bewilderment verbally, "am I missing something here?" she asked. No one responded.

I followed Tom past the control room, through the catering tent, and through the wooden service gate that prevented unauthorised access into the back of the hotel. "Where are we going," I asked him as we walked past the cottage and through the orchard, towards the barn that was supposed to be off limits until Chief Inspector Mokoena had wrapped up his investigation. "You know we can't go in there." I reminded him in a shrill voice that made me sound like a drunken siren.
He ignored me and punched in a security code instead. The heavy metal door slid open, and I followed him in like the zombie I had become. The door slid shut the moment I stepped in, and another door opened revealing the biggest surprise of my lifetime.

Inside the barn there was a quaint eco-home with a small garden with real grass. Jessica was pruning a rose bush. Sammy, Rosemary and Jamie were chatting and merrily sipping on homemade lemonade around a picnic table; seeing them all together made me incredibly thirsty for blood.

"Will someone explain what the hell is going on here?" I roared, spraying fury indiscriminately. They had snapped my last nerve and there was no going back. Sammy got up to explain, but the look on my face stopped him dead in his tracks. Jessica was a lot braver; she came towards me her arms reaching out to hug me; I waved her away angrily. "Don't you even think about touching me," I hissed.

She was her usual persistent self, "I won't touch you if you don't want me to, but will you sit down and let me explain?" she said.

I shrugged and rolled my eyes as I was about to be given another instalment of the truth.

The explosion that occurred the night Koos disappeared was just a smokescreen for Koos' disappearance. Chief Inspector Mokena's forensic investigation had provided the cover for Sammy and Tom to soundproof the barn, install a one way glass roof, and erect the flat pack eco-house inside it. My parents and Rosemary had been seeing the day and night skies through the one-way glass roof since the day we'd had a family lunch in the hotel. A series of high level shenanigans were involved in making the implausible feasible. Exposing Ella and Hamish was as important as the future of the rand to a small group of very powerful people that wanted to shake up the current establishment; they were former revolutionaries and decision makers in politics and economics. They were perceived as pie in the sky eating idealists that welcomed the fruits of liberation, but refused to adapt their beliefs to the reality of freedom.

Tom was the most vocal of these post revolution rebels; he used his media empire to be a thorn on the government's side. He and his former comrades reviled each other publicly, yet they shared cigars and cognac in their private studies. The fallen revolutionaries saw politics as nothing more than a means of keeping the LP ahead of its political opponents. Their private debates with the idealists were entertaining, a nostalgic homage to how far they had come. Their ideology was maintaining control over the wealth that was flowing into their coffers. They addressed few of the nation's urgent needs and focussed on closing the most lucrative deals, which were usually not at the best interests of the country and its people.

At first I didn't understand how uncovering Kwezi could bring the government to its knees, until Sammy explained that Kwezi had bankrolled the LP's campaigns and investments from when the path to the first democratic elections was laid down on foreign soil. She wielded great influence in political circles despite her company's continuing human rights violations. The crimes she once committed against the LP during the liberation struggle would rock the nation, and expose the depths their leaders would sink to for power. Some of her company's drug trials were illicitly conducted in poor areas and facilitated by high-ranking LP health officials. That scandal alone would put the Liberation Party in Hitler's league. The Big Five were working overtime to prevent that catastrophe from happening, and so was Kwezi.

"She's been very busy over the past few weeks; Uncle Victor has no idea who he's dealing with." Sammy was saying when my phone rang.

It was Ella asking me to meet her at a restaurant on the banks of the Vaal River. The news caused a stir; I didn't know which frantic voice to pay attention to because they were all blathering at the same time.

"She's definitely taking you for a short sail; keep your phone close at all times." Tom advised; concern was written all over the deep furrow on his forehead. "Take Tasha with you, after all she's your assistant too, and you don't know your way around well enough." He added with finality.

Tasha was more than pleased to accompany me, "I was starting to feel like canned fruit stewing in that overheated tin of an office," she said as she drove out the gate. She did most of the talking while I drifted in and out of considering what Ella's motives could be. By the time we arrived at our rendezvous, I had heard Tasha's entire life story in snippets. We parked in front of a two storey farmhouse overlooking the Vaal River. The stoep that wrapped around the house was also an outside dining area with an impressive collection of rustic garden furniture.

"This place is amazing," Tasha marvelled once we were on the other side of the stained-glass door.

The inside was softly lit and comfortably furnished; it felt like a rustic living room. A large stone fireplace was the dominant feature in the restaurant. The wooden floors, steel pressed ceilings, Persian rugs, and intimately arranged mixture of antique living room and dining room furniture added to its rural charm.

Ella was sitting on an armchair near the fireplace. She had missed our entrance because she was reading a book with her back to the door. Her feet were propped up on a wooden foot stool; the mug of hot chocolate topped with whipped cream on the side table completed the picture of relaxation. Ella didn't seem to mind Tasha's presence.

She greeted us warmly, and signalled for a waiter to bring two more of what she was having. We drank hot chocolate and made enough small talk to kill twenty minutes and get away with it.

Ella asked to speak to me privately while our meal was being prepared. I excused myself and followed her to her office just as the waiter was returning with a bottle of champagne and a bowl of spicy sweet potato chips for Tasha's amusement. The restaurant was one of Ella's numerous business interests; I later found out that she also owned most of the luxury housing developments along the river.

She led me into the restaurant's kitchen and up a narrow staircase to a door with an electronic lock. We walked straight into an open plan kitchen with black marble worktops and stainless steel shelf doors. She showed me into a stylish living room that was dressed in African and Indonesian furniture, artwork and fabrics.

"This is where I come to get away from it all," she said as she sat on a chaise lounge, patting a spot beside her for me to sit on.

I obliged, looking at her with open curiosity.

"I'm not going to eat you," she chuckled, and then she cleared her throat. "I have a business proposition for you if you don't mind signing a confidentiality contract." She said, glancing pointedly at the document that was lying on the coffee table.

I picked it up, read it, signed it, and gave it to her wordlessly.

"Great: I'd like you to set up discreet cameras in my club and stream the live video data to a remote server via satellite. You'll receive your fee in cash. I don't want a paper trail; this transaction is not happening." She handed me a brown envelope stuffed full of two hundred rand notes, and the buzzer went off as I slipped the envelope into my handbag.

"That must be dinner," she said.

Tasha had already quaffed most of the champagne, "I think you are driving us back," she slurred.

"No problem," I said, laughing at my drunken

"assistant".

"In my world, she'd be looking through the classifieds for work when she sobers up," Ella chuckled despite her obvious disapproval.

Tasha kept us entertained with the risqué version of her epic life story through dinner, dessert and coffee. The drive home was uneventful and relaxing since she had finally passed out, and I could play loud hip-hop in peace. That feeling ended abruptly when I found Sammy and Tom pacing around the driveway occasionally stopping to yell at each other. "I wonder what that is about," I said to no one since Tasha was snoring in a foreign language on the passenger seat.

"I can't do this right now," Sammy was saying when I stepped down from the mud-caked SUV. He started walking towards me and Tom turned and walked away in a huff.

"What's going on now?" I asked.

He drew a slow breath to calm himself down and replied in a stage whisper, "Your father was just unloading his fears for you on me." His sober face became animated as he pointed frantically at something that was behind me. I turned around with a start just in time to see Tasha's vomit cascading down the passenger door; Sammy shook his head disapprovingly, "at least she had the sense to stick her head out." He sounded as disgusted as he looked.

"I can't deal with this right now," I mumbled, and

headed for my cottage with a silent prayer looping in my head. "Please make them all go away," the voice in my head chanted over Sammy's voice calling my name with a tinge of desperation. I ran and only stopped because my body refused to jump into the icy waters of the stream.

"Go for it. If anyone needs a reality check, it's you," said Tom's drunken voice from behind me. He was sprawled on my sun-lounger swigging brandy from the bottle. I sunk to the ground in despair. The mud squelching through the fabric of my trousers through to my knickers put paid to the lows of being Tom and Kwezi's offspring.

"Get me the hell out of here or I'll never speak to you again." I exploded when Sammy helped me up from the mire.

We walked back to the parking lot leaving Tom and his demons behind, only to run into Tasha vomiting into a waste bin outside the mobile office. Eve was on the phone; she waved us over through the window, but Sammy signalled that he'd call her later.

My bottom was caked with dry mud when I stepped under his shower with all my clothes on. I let the water run until it was clear and scrubbed myself down. I was grit-free and dry when I cocooned myself in a slightly big towelling gown and matching slippers. I drank the mug of Horlicks that was on my bedside, and went straight to sleep. Breakfast started with a communication glitch; he was walking on eggs and I felt like an abandoned hatchling. A bolt of clarity came down from out of nowhere, blinding me with fresh perspective.

"We shouldn't even consider the possibility of being together; it's too messy.' I announced when his cook had gone back to the kitchen with our empty cereal bowls. He started to argue, but I ensured him that it would never work. We went back to being two hungry people with a fry up between them.

"If you ever change your mind, let me know," he said.

I nodded in agreement; partly because my mouth was too full, but mostly because I had already locked the door to a future with him, realised it would be impossible to erase his fantasy over one breakfast sitting, so I left the sliver of hope linger.

We entered the hotel through the back gate, which was a first for me. The sombre mood in the barn gave way to an outbreak of activity when we arrived. Tom was bleary eyed and sulky, but he was in a much better state than the night before. We sat around the picnic table pretending there was nothing amiss between Tom and Sammy. I avoided Rosemary's stricken eyes as we plotted our next move with Jessica buzzing around us like a worker bee on steroids, feeding us tit bits of her vegan delicacies. Ella had paid for quick service; we wanted to ensure that she got that and more.

Yet again Sammy's influence proved to be a pre-emptive advantage, enabling us to pull an inconspicuous Indian technical genius out of his magic hat. He preferred to be called "Jazz" and he could talk a mole out of the ground. I had to extricate him from a giggly group of students when I picked him up from a coffee shop not far from Ella's club. It was not difficult to spot the face I had seen in a picture the day before. His slightly longer hair and the fashionable outcrop of stubble were the only things that had changed. I settled his table's bill before approaching him; the cashier seemed bemused but she did not argue.

"I'm in a hurry," I explained. My unsolicited clarification earned me another look of utter consternation. The cashier was a middle-aged Goth with jet black hair and red lips that were fixed in a plump pout. Jazz recognised me and got up, so I lingered at the counter while he planted a kiss on each girl's cheek.

"Your change," said the cashier.

"Thanks, you can keep it," I smiled. Her plump red lips stretched against her taut face into a surprised smile.

"Someone must put her cosmetic surgeon to sleep before he brutalises another soul," said Jazz once we are outside. I tittered. "I'm jazz, but I'm sure you already know that, or you wouldn't be here." He said.

"Nice meeting you Jazz; do you think you can shut up when you get to the job?" I asked feeling annoyed and panicky.

His boyish face cracked into a smile, "don't stress. Sammy doesn't work with amateurs; you can trust me."

"We'll be late if we don't leave now," I replied, walking briskly to where the car was parked. Ella's gate slid open when we stopped in front of it. I drove in and parked where Sammy's driver would have. This time Ella came out to meet us and led us into the house. A stunner of a maid was already waiting at the door to take Jazz's overnight bag upstairs; he would spend two nights at the club as a paying guest. Ella's part was to ascertain that he had enough privacy to go about his business undisturbed. Jazz's transformation from outgoing motor mouth to thoughtful nerd was nothing short of incredible. I had a drink with them and then I excused myself, citing the long drive alone.

"Why don't you spend the night with your beau," Ella suggested mischievously.

"It's complicated," I replied, faking lightness despite the weight in my heart when I thought of Sammy in that way. I had no idea how long it would take me to fall out of love with him, but I hoped that with time thinking about him would hurt less.

"Maybe you can tell me all about it when I come over for lunch." She offered as we hugged goodbye.

"I'd much rather not if you don't mind," I replied.

I was ahead of the afternoon traffic that snaked out of the city in all directions, so I drove as fast as I legally could. It was only three days before wrap, and life was crazier than usual. There was a huge party to plan; thankfully Tasha had left that to highly paid professionals that feared her too much to disappoint her. She had also put together an experienced Public Relations team to handle the live press conference that would precede the staff exiting the house. All I had to worry about was looking human, and what to cook for lunch with Ella.

She had booked a room at a luxury spa nearby so she could spend the rest of the afternoon getting pampered for the party, which was scheduled to start at the stroke of midnight.
Needless to say, cooking was the least of my worries. I hoped I could stay calm and natural long enough for Ella and me to be able to take a leisurely walk on the grounds after lunch.

"I have butterflies and wasps fighting for real estate in my stomach," Eve confessed as she rinsed our coffee mugs in the sink.

"I'll swap places with you if you like," I replied, wishing the day away.

"I can't wait to have my friends back," she said dreamily. She had lost me for a moment; I had not expected her feelings for Justina, Alana and Abe to be that strong.

"I doubt they'll want anything to do with us commoners now that they are international celebrities." I joked.

"Don't tempt fate, even Alana may just see greener pastures after all the attention she'll be getting," she scoffed. We walked together as far as the vegetable garden, where I stayed behind to pick carrots and herbs for lunch. It was a good thing I started early because Ella arrived at noon on the dot, sending her driver back to Johannesburg to pick up her dress.

"You look less frantic than I expected you to be considering the circumstances" she had said hugging me. She smelled like a field of jasmine after a spring shower.

"I'd introduce you to the crew, but today everyone is on edge. It's as bad as the first day," I said. There was no one out on a smoke break; even the security detail seemed extra alert.

"You should take a drive down the road; Parys is like Ibiza in summer. It took my driver over thirty minutes to make it out of that one horse town." She was good at filling uncomfortable communication gaps with small talk. I was grateful to her gift of the gab, since Eve's butterflies and wasps were using my stomach for a fresh bout of their territorial war. "Are you sure you made all of this?" she waved a manicured had over the dishes I was taking out of the warmer.

After agonising over what to cook I had settled for a buffet of bobotie, grilled haddock topped with stilton and crumbs, Greek salad and roast vegetables. I uncorked her favourite champagne and we toasted to "living". She took our plates to the deck so we could soak up the bright winter sun, and I followed her out with the drinks.

"Do you know if the owner is selling?" Ella enquired

casually when I returned from the kitchen with warm chocolate and walnut brownies topped with homemade vanilla ice cream.

I pulled a face, "sorry, but I've already made them an offer they couldn't refuse."

She savoured a spoonful of dessert with her eyes closed, "this is sinfully good." She marvelled with a satisfied grin.

"I'll give you the recipe for the brownies after I've shown you around the grounds." I smiled sweetly to cover my lie.

"I'll help you with washing up," she offered.

I declined and suggested we take a basket to fill it with whatever she wanted instead. We started out in the vegetable gardens, then we moved from the herbs to the orchard, but for a reason unbeknownst to me I couldn't let her into the hothouse. "Let's visit the barn first and save the greenhouse for last," I suggested.
I led her away from my haven towards the jagged edges of her past. Ella gasped when the lights came on after the door had slid shut behind us.

"I Knew there was something familiar about you; I just couldn't put a finger on it," she said after taking deep breaths for composure.

"It's a sad day when a woman can't recognise a picture of her former self," I replied. "Shall we join the others?" I added courteously.

The men were playing cards on the picnic bench, and the women were side by side on sun-loungers chatting boredom away. Jessica was knitting furiously, which was a warning sign with flashing lights. Ella did not recognise her cousin, but Rosemary could still see Kwezi beneath all the cosmetic surgery. Her features may have been altered, but she could see Kwezi in Ella's smaller slanted eyes.

Ella didn't know Jessica and Jamie from a bar of perfumed soap; it was Tom and Sammy's presence that got her alarms whirring. She marched past the women regarding them with a curt nod. She only had words for Sammy.

"So I am right, it's you that's pulling Victor's strings," she said. "I did a thorough check on her and I found nothing." She announced, jerking her head in my direction. "Kudos to you and your protégé, you've gotten better at the art of deception."

Tom had had enough of her and the way he addressed her betrayed his impatience. "Sit down. There's really no need for you to work yourself up; we are all family here. Besides your help is not coming because your tracking device says you are en route to India, and the last entry in your diary confirms that." He couldn't bring himself to look at her for long enough to see into her eyes.

She took the proffered seat reluctantly, "what do you want Sizwe?" she asked, trying to meet his faraway gaze.

He looked into her eyes for the first time since we'd walked in; she was not ready for what she saw in his. "Your freedom," he replied, emotionless.

She studied our faces intently, and then her eyes rested on me for what seemed like an eternity. "So, she's alive and my father has disappeared; how interesting," she addressed Tom without looking at him. "What do you want for me to get my father back?" she asked looking at Sammy.

He shook his head, "He's already given me what I want, and now you are here. What more could I ask for?"

That's when it struck me that just like Tom he hated Kwezi more for making it hard for him to trust in love than all the vile acts she had committed. He went into the house and remerged with an old man that could have only been my grandfather. Beneath the beard was a faintly weather beaten face with the familiar eyes I had learnt to avoid. They softened when they rested on his daughters. My mother stayed put, but Kwezi ran over to him and they hugged for a long time. Jessica's knitting needles collided frantically, clanking with disproval.

"I take it we can move on to more relevant matters now that the touching reunion is out of the way." She had said, packing her knitting away.

Kwezi extricated herself from the hug, glancing at her father then Jessica like someone watching a game of tennis. She wore her pain and bewilderment on her sleeve as her mind picked at the faint resemblance between Hamish and her half-sister.

"How many other secrets are you keeping from me?" she asked him, her voice quivering.

"We are all entitled to a few secrets. If Bella and I cannot tell you everything it's not betrayal, its love. That's what parents do; sometimes they sacrifice the truth to protect their children." He replied.

"She doesn't know, does she?" Jessica piped in as she took her place beside Jamie on the picnic bench.

Kwezi glared at her, "I can see the resemblance, which means now I know," she replied in her father's place.

Jessica cracked a cheerless smile, "what did he do to the poor girl?" she wondered out loud.

Hamish found his tongue, "do me a favour; stay out of this one." He said.

Jessica guffawed. "You are asking the wrong person for a favour. Fighting the urge to vomit on you these past weeks has taken a lot out of me," she snarled.

Jamie looked up from the card game for the first time since Kwezi entered the barn, "let's just play the recording and stop this bickering," he said.

Like sheep, we all followed him into the living room. The video was recorded in what seemed to be an office. It was an unusual sight; Hamish was flanked by the minister of justice and two high ranking police

officers, one of whom was Mokoena. My grandfather made his full confession of all his crimes including the thousands of people he had bought, used and discarded over four decades. He provided details and evidence on how he had been creating and providing biological weapons to the highest bidders, giving a longer lease to the lives of super powers, dictators and white collar criminals. He came clean about murdering Susan, and how Bella had had Momo killed to protect their nefarious interests. He had spoken the whole truth, implicated everyone that had played a hand in the dark side of his bio-technology and pharmaceuticals empire.
His entire family would go down with him, even Isabella. Her cosmetics company had gone to inhumane lengths to pioneer placenta masks and other miracle beauty potions. The most shocking revelation for my mother was the details of his designer-baby programme.

As much as I disapproved of Kwezi, it pained me to see how Hamish had violated her more than the rest of us could ever claim to have been damaged. Until that day she had believed that Angel died giving birth to her. It had never occurred to her that Momo, Jessica and herself had been the first successful phase of the Centurion Genome Project.

"You should have told me." She said, devoid of emotion. It was only then that it occurred to her that her existence had been dreamed up by two young scientists whose creativity was matched only by their fearlessness. Despite everything Kwezi had learned about heredity, she had never questioned the fact that her eyes were identical to those of the baby girl in the picture she once found Bella crying over soon after Hamish had left her. It was that child's death that made them decide to have other women carry their designer-embryos.

"Who decided what traits I would inherit from you, Bella's child and the unfortunate woman that carried me to full-term?" she asked, unsure of herself for the first time since I'd met her.

Hamish shrugged, "Bella and me love you as much as we love Isabella..."

"I think you love me as much as you loved Momo, that's probably why I'm the one that had to pay the man that sabotaged her plane." She sneered.

"I'm sorry I wasn't around to clean up my own mess-" he started explaining away his unforgivable actions, but Kwezi had had enough.

"You and mama should have kept us in your laboratory like the experiments we are, instead of dragging us into your mess. Did you program us to be as ruthless as you are?" she spat a column of fire directed at Hamish.

His hands were trembling, "I've done some terrible things in my lifetime, but I did not ask you to kill your sister; I wouldn't do that to any of my children. Watching you all grow-up is part of the reason I ended up here; let's just say being a father softened me to the reality of my actions." He let out a drawn out sigh.

She shook her head and said, "Now we have to pay for your sins because you seek redemption."

Hamish tried to close the space that was growing between them, but she moved back as he inched closer. "I'm sorry my love, but we all have to pay for our individual crimes. I didn't make you choose to work with me. I made you sign non-disclosure agreements and explained everything to you when you and your sisters came to me us work; as for your mama; she's always known that a day like this would come." He fell silent and sank into a chair, wiping the sweat off his brow.

"You took away our choices when you betrayed us. Mama and Isabella will never forgive you, nor will I" She said the words with finality, without emotion.

"I owed Alana the truth," he said. For his love for Alana and his need to be respected by her, he had given up his entire life.

"Who's Alana?" she asked, scanning our eyes.

"She's the cook in the show; his wife," I answered since no one else would.
She laughed clutching at the seat of the chair to steady herself.

"What now?" Hamish asked.

## THE END

All the guests had checked in by ten that night. Johannesburg's glamorous types turned up in full swing, primed for the red carpet and the flashing lights. Everyone was waiting with baited breath for the stars of Hotel Parys to come out; the guests milled around in the huge marquee that covered the front lawn. It was like being in the inside of a ballroom with a giant screen that filled an entire wall. Waiters in tuxedos served champagne and hors de oeuvres from silver trays and a string quartet was playing on the gazebo. Suddenly the music died, and Joy Khanya's familiar voice boomed out of the speakers. My first day in Johannesburg came crashing back like an acid flashback; Joy's "kidnapping" was one of the threads that were woven into bringing that day to be.

"What you are about to witness is the beginning of the biggest anti-corruption raid ever!" said Joy's disembodied voice.

All the eyes in the makeshift room turned to the image of the kitchen door on the big screen; even Uncle Victor was beaming with excitement, waiting for that door to burst open. The door did fly open but no one sprang out, instead the world was treated to Hamish's confession. Leading figures in the Liberation Party inched towards the doorway as he made public the huge donations and dealings that tied him to the LP. Jazz then streamed the raw video footage he had retrieved from Ella's server; it was of her last meeting with the Big Five and Uncle Victor. The world heard them incriminate each other in their own words.

Kwezi was standing between me and Thomas with Sammy behind her at the front of the room; there was no going anywhere else.

"That's not what I paid you for," she spat at me. I didn't blame her; that was the confession she was planning to use to cut and paste herself into a saint.

We stayed up all night, surfing channels watching the stream of news as the web unfolded. Arrests were made in stately homes and grotty flats around the world. The dear old couple that had sold me the hotel was arrested en-route to Switzerland. For almost a week the world remained transfixed as lies collapsed revealing dreadful truths.

"I want to say goodbye to him," Alana said the evening before Hamish and Kwezi were to be shipped to another country.

"I'm sorry Alana." I said, squeezing her tiny hand.

"Did you make me marry a gardener I had just met while I was on a holiday with my fiancé?" she asked.

As each day passed I woke up to a better world, somehow grateful to my grandfather for encoding good health, intelligence and a long life into my genes. I was finally free, so I stayed in Parys and made an imperfect but fulfilling life for myself.